UNCLAIMED BAGGAGE

UNCLAIMED BAGGAGE

KATIE O'ROURKE

This is a work of fiction. Names, characters, places, and incidents either are the product of the author's imagination or are used fictitiously. Any resemblance to actual persons, living or dead, events, or locales is entirely coincidental.

Copyright © 2025 by Katie O'Rourke

Library of Congress Cataloging-in-Publication Data

Names: O'Rourke, Katie, 1978–, author.
Title: Unclaimed Baggage / Katie O'Rourke
206 pages. – First edition.
Description: Laguna Hills, California: Type Eighteen Books, 2025.
  | Summary: "When an incurable people pleaser leaves college to become caretaker to her ailing stepfather, a family secret crashes into her already complicated life; she is forced to navigate grief and betrayal-all while falling for the first good man she has ever dated." –Provided by publisher.
Identifiers: LCCN 2025930592 | ISBN: 979-8-992-04050-0 (paperback) | ISBN: 979-8-992-04051-7 (ebook)
LC record available at https://lccn.loc.gov/2025930592

Published by Type Eighteen Books
www.typeeighteenbooks.com

Printed in the United States

Also by Katie O'Rourke

Blood & Water
Finding Charlie
Still Life and Other Stories
A Long Thaw
Monsoon Season

Chapter One

"You awake?"

"Mm-hmm." Surfacing, Jenna tries to remind herself of her surroundings. She's in bed with a man. A man, though not a heterosexual one. It has been years since that happened. She was still a kid then, sneaking out the basement window of her parents' house, fumbling with buttons, rushing to get home before anyone knew she was gone. Had she ever slept with a man the whole night through?

Beside her, Liam is sobbing, his curly black chest hair poking out the collar of his white T-shirt. He's certainly a man, but it's not the same. Jenna has never understood women who are attracted to gay men. Lying next to her, he could be her father, her brother, her son. Sexually speaking, they're two positively charged magnets naturally pushing away from one another. For altogether different reasons, they haven't been sleeping through the night together either.

"I'm here," Jenna says. She glances at the clock. 4:02. She slept for about an hour. There's still no light piercing through the slats of the Venetian blinds. Jenna wants to paint the walls, but they're renting. She thinks she may be able to charm the landlord, but she hasn't worked up the nerve yet. For now, she settles for the bland off-white and considers covering them with posters. They're still getting settled.

Liam sits up. Jenna puts her hand on his back and feels the quiet sobs shaking his body. "I'm sorry," he says.

"It's okay, it's fine." Jenna yawns. She already forgot what she was dreaming about. Something about trying on shoes. Or maybe ice skates. "What are you thinking about now?"

"That I haven't slept at all, and I have to get ready for work in two hours." He gulps. "And I'm scared." He begins to sob again.

It has been like this for weeks now. Since Liam started his new job. It was his idea for them to move in together. Jenna was starting her senior year of college. Liam, a year ahead, was beginning his life as a grown-up. They toasted to his first day of work on a Sunday night two weeks ago. And Liam hasn't slept more than two hours a night since. Jenna's getting there.

"How many pills have you taken?" Jenna asks.

"Two."

After the first week, Jenna went with him to Urgent Care, where they prescribed him Xanax and gave him free samples of Zoloft. The Zoloft sits untouched in the medicine cabinet as he weighs the pros and cons of antidepressants. The Xanex seems to have less and less effect.

"Alphabet game?" Jenna asks.

"Okay." Liam leans back against the pillows and forces his eyes shut. "What topic?"

"States." Jenna settles into her pillow, closing her eyes with relief. She has never been able to function on fewer than eight hours of sleep. She prefers ten. She's already trying to think if she has time to fit a nap in between classes.

Liam rattles off Alabama, Alaska, Arizona, and Arkansas. He doesn't get stuck until the O's, pausing for several minutes. Long enough for Jenna to drift off.

"Oregon," he says at last, and Jenna jumps, reminding herself all over again where she is, and that this is her life.

***

Currently, about an inch stands between Jenna and true happiness.

The week before, in preparation for the start of the fall semester, Jenna got a haircut and—due to a slight miscommunication—ended up with bangs. The last time she had bangs she was in the third grade. She remembers trying to stick it out past the awkward stage when they fell into her eyes, weeks of using bobby pins and hair spray before finally giving up and getting them trimmed. She had them *feathered* in fifth grade, in time for class pictures, preserving the evidence for all time. By her sixth-grade picture, her hair finally returned to normal: Flat and brown, parted in the middle. Since then, she has always been keenly aware her level of happiness depends on her ability to tuck her hair behind her ears.

Jenna explained all this to the hairdresser as she always did. She sat in the chair with her feet on the metal bar, wrapped in a black plastic cape. Her hair slid down the cape and onto the floor around her. *Inches.* She'd said she wanted a change.

The hairdresser talked to Jenna with a comb between her lips. Asked where she worked. Does she go to school or have a boyfriend? Jenna likes it better when they don't talk. The best hairdresser she ever had didn't speak English well and had long, blood-red fingernails. With her, Jenna kept her eyes closed, soothed by the quiet and the sensation of those nails on her scalp.

Last week, there was a moment when Jenna knew she could have stopped it. She saw the scissors were too high. She held her breath and reminded herself hair grows back. She said nothing. She didn't want to be difficult.

But it is my hair, she thinks now, uselessly, as she searches for a headband.

On that day, Jenna smiled. Nodded. Paid. Went to work.

Jenna could have stopped her, but she didn't. The truth of the matter is, she was complicit.

***

Jenna's cell phone rings on her walk to class. It's a bright, still warm September day. The grass has been recently cut and maintains its color. Jenna shifts her bag to the front of her body and continues walking as she pulls the silver flip phone from a zippered pocket. The number flashing belongs to her sister.

"It's Bill," Julie says in a rush, skipping the hello.

"Bill?" Jenna shifts her bag higher on her shoulder.

"Dad," she says, meaning their stepfather—the only man they refer to this way.

Having several Bills in her life is confusing. Jenna's father, the one her mother refers to as, "the biological," lives in Pennsylvania with his mutually born-again wife and their two sons. Jenna isn't sure if the boys have had time to be born a second time yet. She only sees them once a year, in the summer when she and her sister make their obligatory bus visit. Then there's her older brother Bill, sometimes called Billy to make things easier, in medical school in Chicago. Her stepfather, the man who had raised her since she was six, is also Bill. As is his son from his previous marriage—her stepbrother—who lives in some sort of Buddhist commune in Vermont. Talking about the men in her life could be like the old "Who's on First?" routine.

"What about him?" Jenna asks this casually, but her heart is thumping loudly in her ears.

"He's in the hospital again."

"What happened?" Jenna sits on a bench, wondering if this will be a crisis worthy of missing her three afternoon classes or whether it will make her late for the next one. She hates being late, hates the way everyone's head turns to acknowledge her sneaking in. The apologetic, sheepish shrug she will give as she takes a seat in the back row.

"He was dizzy and talking crazy again. I could barely get him to the car by myself. Thought I was going to have to call an ambulance."

"What are the doctors saying?"

"They're running tests. He probably needs another transfusion. He was asleep when I left."

"Where's Mom?"

"Cincinnati, I think. Business."

"Shouldn't someone be with him?"

"Duh. That's why I'm calling you."

"Julie!"

"What? You know I hate hospitals."

"You hate everything." Julie's hospital phobia has been especially unhelpful these last two years while Bill's been sick. Jenna sighs, hitching her bag to her shoulder again and changing course, walking toward the parking lot. "On my way," she says, snapping the phone shut.

When Jenna and Julie were small, they'd been fluent in their own language, their own world of understanding that shut everyone else out. Their mother would hesitate in doorways as they chattered with each other. When she walked in, often the girls fell silent, as if their twin-speak was the subject of a top-secret government mission.

They were the embodiment of the word *symbiosis*. They'd slept in the same womb for nine months, spooning in a fleshy sack. They'd whispered into each other's ears as they formed.

And yet, twenty-one years later, it seems unimaginable to Jenna that they ever had a common language, or they had understood each other at all, never mind *best*.

Driving fast, Jenna can get from her school in Massachusetts to the hospital in New Hampshire in under an hour and a half. When she gets there, Bill's asleep, making her question the point of rushing. He sleeps most of the day. Every time he wakes up, he acts pleasantly surprised to find Jenna there, sitting in the uncomfortable plastic and metal chair by his bedside. He talks to her for a few minutes and falls back to sleep. She leaves him for half an hour to eat dinner in the cafeteria. She speaks to his doctor, nodding in all the right places, trying to take it all in.

While he sleeps, she considers taking his hand but decides not to wake him. It isn't that he looks peaceful; he has a deep groove between his eyebrows, scowling at his dreams. She doesn't know whether he'll be making sense, and when he loses grasp of reality, it's scary. There's no telling what he might say, who he'll be. Once, he said something racist to a nurse—something he would never say if he were himself. Something, Jenna's certain, he would never even think.

Bill was sixty-five when he was diagnosed with heart valve failure. He was fourteen years older than her mother, but no one believed it. His age caught up to him after the first heart surgery, though. He lost all his color, turning a cadaver-like gray that never went away. If Jenna caught him napping, which started happening more and more often, she had to check his chest was rising in the labored way that was frightening and reassuring all at once.

"Jenna." The nurse comes in and smiles. "How's it going?"

Jenna sits up in her chair. "You tell me."

The nurse checks his IV. Looks at his chart. "Hangin' in, I'd say. He's a tough guy."

Jenna nods and the nurse leaves. After the second surgery, the doctors said his body couldn't take another. They gave him a few months. That was almost a year ago.

Bill stirs. He must have heard the voices. Jenna leans forward and takes his hand as he blinks at her and tries to orient himself among the stiff, white sheets and pastel, patterned draperies.

"Jenna," he says and his face lights up with recognition.

"Hey," she says softly. "How are you feeling?"

He looks around the room. A dated floral border runs along the top edge of the walls, nothing like home. Jenna's mother has always found them tacky. "Tired." He sighs.

"Why don't you go back to sleep then?" Jenna smiles, encouragingly.

The smell is the clearest indication of where they are, so clean it nearly burns your lungs.

"Where's Julie?" he asks, and Jenna feels an old stab of jealousy. When their mother had started dating Bill, the twins were five and already veering off in their own directions, but united in their refusal to give him a chance. Julie had been the first to give in to his persistent offer of friendship. Back then, Jenna thought she would never forgive her sister. But after Bill won Jenna over as well, she found herself resenting that Julie had been the first to let him love her.

"She stepped out," Jenna answers. "She'll be back later."

"Is it late?"

Jenna looks at her watch. "Nine-fifteen."

"You should get back to school. You have a long drive."

"It's okay, Bill." She loves the feeling of him worrying about her, being paternal. These moments have become so rare.

Bill closes his eyes. "I'm going to sleep now. You go."

***

It's after eleven when Jenna gets back to the apartment. All the lights are out, but there's a soft glow coming down the hall from the back bedroom. *Her bedroom.* She knows Liam's waiting for her there, and she wishes she could go to sleep without having to talk to him. It's been such a long day and all she wants is quiet.

Which is selfish, she thinks to herself. Liam is her friend, and he needs her. She pours herself a glass of water, standing in front of the short slab of mustard-colored Formica passing for a kitchen counter, delaying the inevitable.

"Where have you been?"

She turns to find him standing behind her, barefoot, hugging a pillow like an eight-year-old with a teddy bear.

"I'm sorry," she says. "I forgot to call. I was at the hospital."

"The hospital?"

Jenna sighs. "Come on. Let's go to bed."

He follows her down the hall. She sets her water glass on the night table and goes into the bathroom to pee. "My dad's sick again," she says from the toilet. "Nothing new. He'll probably go home tomorrow."

"Are you going home again?"

Jenna isn't sure. "Hopefully, my sister can handle it. But you know her." Julie was born second and takes her place as the baby in the family very seriously.

Jenna kicks off her shoes and her pants. She flushes the toilet and thinks about brushing her teeth, but she's too tired. She walks back into the bedroom wearing her T-shirt.

"Your sister's a bitch," Liam says.

"Hey. Don't say that. Just." She shakes her head. "Don't."

"Sorry."

Jenna gets under the covers. How can she explain the way it assaults her to hear someone speak badly of her sister? Even if they're right. Even if she thinks the same thing. Jenna taught Julie how to tie her shoelaces. She held her hand everywhere they went for years, did the talking for them both. Julie was always a little smaller, shy. Jenna took care of her. Jenna always felt like Julie was *hers*.

"My day," Liam says, sitting up with his head in his hand, "was awful."

"What happened?" Jenna reaches for the light switch, but she stops, letting her hand fall into her lap.

"I stand up there in front of them all day, and I know they can tell I'm a fraud!"

"Liam, they're five-year-olds."

Liam is teaching kindergarten.

"I know, I *know*." He squeezes his eyes shut. "There's this canyon of space between what I know and how I feel. You know what I mean?"

She does know what he means. It's like worrying about Bill doesn't change anything. And knowing that doesn't make her worry any less.

"Uh-huh. Can I shut the light out? You can still talk, but my eyes are tired."

Liam sighs. "Okay."

The first night, he shook her awake and begged to lie down beside her. He said he felt so alone. He needed to feel someone near him, even asleep. She was a heavy sleeper. She wouldn't even notice him. It was something that would help him and cost her nothing. How could she refuse?

Then, night after night, he appeared at her door with his pillow. Earlier and earlier, until finally he was going to bed before her—in her room.

"Jenna?"

"Mm-hmm."

"I'm scared."

"I know. It'll be okay."

"It will?"

"Yeah."

***

Jenna helps Bill up the front steps of the house. He grips the railing with one hand and her arm with the other. She has an arm around his waist, and she can feel how small he has become, how fragile.

He sits in his favorite chair in the den and asks for the remote. Norman, their cocker spaniel, wags excitedly at his feet. Norman loves Bill the best, to the near exclusion of anyone else, and hates it when Bill has to go away for a night. He doesn't understand.

Bill rubs Norman's ears as Jenna switches the television on and hands him the remote. He likes to watch *The View*, she knows, and it's almost over.

"Norman, don't be a pest," she says, but he ignores her, basking in the glow of Bill's attention.

"He's okay," Bill says in a lilting sing-song Jenna has grown to think of as doggy-talk. He's missed Norman just as much.

Jenna walks down the hall to the kitchen, talking over her shoulder. "What do you want to drink?"

There's a pause and Jenna can hear the changing of channels. "A ginger ale?"

"Okay." Jenna opens a can and pours the soda over ice. She counts out his meds. Through the window, she sees her mother's car pulling into the driveway.

"Mom's home." Jenna sets his drink on the table beside him and transfers his pills carefully into his palm.

"Is she home early?" Bill takes the pills in one gulp and chases them with the ginger ale.

"I'm not sure." Jenna hasn't spoken to her mother in days. This morning, when Julie bailed on bringing Bill home, she tried calling her mother's cell phone but got her voicemail. Jenna had been so angry she didn't leave a message. Now she realizes the phone was probably off because her mother was on a flight home. She feels guilty for not assuming as much.

The screen door bangs. "Where's my little turtle?"

They had started calling him that because of the gray-green pallor of his skin the way he disappears into his clothes. It was funnier when they thought it was temporary. Now, it feels like part of the optimism charade.

"In here!" Bill calls, brightly. He smooths the hair on top of his head.

Barbara comes to the door wearing a long black skirt and a dark magenta wrap. She's wearing full makeup, and when she kisses Bill's forehead, she follows by rubbing the lipstick off with her thumb.

Barbara's makeup gets heavier as she ages. She never wore makeup when the girls were small. Jenna remembers the novelty on the nights when she first started going out with Bill. She set her hair in rollers and sprayed herself with perfume. She painted her lips a shade that probably wasn't quite right for her. The only tube of lipstick she owned then, it still had the new, little slant after years. It was always at the back of the bathroom drawer, behind the Q-tips and Band Aids and other, generally useful things. She left the house looking like a movie star, leaving a fancy smell behind her as proof she'd been there.

She unwinds herself from her wrap and lounges on the couch with her elbows on the arm and her chin on top of her hands. She looks Bill over. "Well, honey, you look fine."

Jenna thinks this is a stretch.

"I am, I am," Bill insists, puffing out his chest. "Just had a spell yesterday. Nothing to worry about."

Barbara tosses her head back and laughs. "You hear that?" she says to Jenna. "Nothing to worry about. What a relief." She pats Bill's hand, beaming at him.

As Jenna walks back to the kitchen, she can hear them bickering about whether she should have cut her trip short. Bill insists it wasn't necessary. Jenna hears her mother say she would have been no use to anyone while she was worried for him. She wouldn't have felt better until she saw for herself that he was fine.

Jenna opens the refrigerator and looks for a snack. Affixed to the freezer is a picture of the twins from first grade. This was the last year the girls were in the same class, the year before Julie was held back. The picture shows Julie with her white-blond hair, wearing a pink parka with faux-fur trim, smiling sweetly, in a dress of pastel flowers and white tights, clean at the knees. Jenna is wearing gray corduroy pants and heavy black winter boots, a navy-blue jacket, unzipped. She appears to be sneering at the camera, but Jenna would say it's more of a wariness, confusion at being photographed without warning. Her brown hair is frizzy in a misguided attempt at a perm. It was the eighties.

"You must be fraternal."

That's the first thing anyone ever says when they're introduced as twins. They look less alike now than in the picture. Julie is blonder—although she gets her hair colored at the salon, and for all Jenna knows, it might be the same mousy brown as her own. If you look closely, they have the same lake-blue eyes, the full mouth too dramatic for lipstick. But this isn't what people tend to see. Julie's eyebrows are tweezed higher and smaller. Julie wears kitten heels with peep toes while Jenna wears flip flops. A 36C, Julie loves trying on lingerie. They don't carry Jenna's size in Victoria's Secret. Or, at least, they didn't the day Julie dragged her along, assuring her she'd have fun. She didn't.

Jenna closes the refrigerator and rummages through the cabinets. There's nothing to eat in the house. She finds half a bag of potato chips in the back of the pantry. She gets herself a soda and sits at the kitchen table.

Jenna's shaped like her mother, who's shaped like *her* mother. Grammy calls their physique "upside-down-pear-shaped." Julie seems to have escaped this legacy. There was a brief period in high school when Jenna thought she might as well. She got an inch taller over summer vacation and suddenly the only thing the boys noticed was her generous amount of cleavage. By the next year, however, she had filled out, and that was that.

Barbara tiptoes down the hall. "Fell asleep," she says quietly. She sits at the table across from her daughter and sighs heavily.

"Tired?" Jenna pushes the bag of chips across the table.

Barbara nods and pops a chip into her mouth. "I don't know how much longer I can keep this up."

"Mom?" Jenna's startled by this admission, the lack of sugar-coating.

"Things are gearing up at work. I keep having to leave. And he's doing worse and worse."

Barbara has always worked in sales. When Bill retired, he helped her start her own business, promoting a certain brand of air filtration system. She sells on a broad scale to hospitals, schools, and museums. It's the kind of job Jenna has trouble explaining to other people. Her mother doesn't create anything or provide a tangible service; it's her job to convince people of an idea. She's still in sales, but now she's the president, traveling around the country to see her sales reps. As far as Jenna can tell, Barbara is the middleman.

Jenna sits with her shoulders hunched, not sure what to say. She wants to argue the point but can't.

"Things were much easier when you were home this summer." Barbara leans her elbows on the table, resting her chin on her hands.

"Is Julie helping at all?" Jenna asks.

"Of course. She keeps him company when she can. But she has a new boyfriend, you know."

Jenna shakes her head. She has a difficult time keeping up with Julie's ever-changing line of suitors. "Is she still working at the clothing store in the mall?"

Barbara cringes. "I'm not sure what happened. She didn't want to talk about it."

"She's not working? What does she do all day?"

"She's looking, I guess. Don't be so hard on her. She's having a tough time with all this."

"Aren't we all?" Jenna leans back in her chair, furious. "I've missed two days of classes so I could be here with Bill."

"That's what families do, Jenna Marie."

Jenna feels stung. Her face flushes with shame. "I'm not complaining," she says, quickly. "I don't see why Julie isn't helping more."

"Julie's not as tough as you are honey. And I think she's been a little lost lately. You should talk to her."

Jenna nods. "You have no food," she says after a minute.

"I keep meaning to go to the store. There's a list on the fridge. Could you go?"

"Me?"

"Well, I'd go myself, but I don't want to leave your dad."

"I have a class at two o 'clock."

"I thought you said you were missing your classes today."

"Well, I thought." Jenna pauses to consider. "Since you're home now."

Jenna's mother looks at her, blankly.

"Okay. I'll go."

"Thanks, honey." Barbara gets up and kisses Jenna's forehead. She rolls up the potato chip bag. "Pick up something easy for dinner. Maybe one of those pre-cooked chickens?" She pulls some cash from her purse. "It'll be nice to have both my girls home for dinner."

"I have to get back to school eventually."

Barbara frowns. "We may not have many more nights to eat dinner as a family."

***

"I don't know how much longer I can keep this up." Liam is pacing through the apartment, wailing hysterically.

Jenna looks up from the computer, unsure her attention is helping him. It seems to feed the fire. She reads the line she's written a second time and a third, unable to follow her own logic. Liam retches loudly in the bathroom. She closes the document, and when Microsoft asks if she'd like to save her work, she hesitates.

"What does it matter?" she says.

She walks to the bathroom and knocks on the door. "You okay in there?"

Liam opens the door and falls into her arms. She manages to lead him to the couch. He's having trouble catching his breath.

"Come on. Deep breath." Jenna rubs his back. She can feel every notch of his spine.

"I think." Liam gasps, rubbing his palms along the top of his thighs. "I have to." Another gasp. "Quit."

"Quit?"

Liam nods.

"Have you talked to your therapist about this?"

Jenna went with Liam to his first appointment with Dr. Mackie. She brought a notebook, and a list of questions Liam was too frantic to remember. When Liam faltered as he described his symptoms, Jenna pitched in. At some point, Liam blew his nose into a Kleenex while she and the doctor discussed him as if he were Jenna's child.

"Not yet," Liam says now.

At first, Jenna thought the therapist was a bit kooky himself. He was in his late thirties, bearded and wore socks with his Birkenstock sandals. Liam and Jenna entered the office feeling exhausted and desperate. They sat together on a low couch with their knees level to their chests, a stick of incense burning on a table. Perhaps it was only in comparison to their fatigue that Dr. Mackie came across as overly caffeinated. He went through a checklist of questions on a worksheet and said, "Congratulations! You're clinically depressed!" But as the appointment went on, he talked about the causes and possible treatments for anxiety disorders. He seemed to know what he was talking about. Besides, the idea of going through everything all over again with another therapist felt impossible.

"Are you still thinking about taking the Zoloft?" Jenna asks.

Liam shrugs.

Dr. Mackie was against using medication as a quick fix. He wanted to try other treatments first. Diet and exercise. Breathing techniques. Journaling. Liam had put Post-its around the apartment to challenge his destructive thought patterns. The one on the bathroom mirror reads: *You are good enough just the way you are.*

"Maybe you could take a medical leave."

"Maybe."

"But it seems like the job isn't the only thing causing the anxiety. It's the change. So quitting the job won't really solve the problem."

Liam nods. "I talked to my mother today. She thinks I should move home."

"To Connecticut?"

"It's where I feel safest. No offense."

Jenna smiles. "It's okay. I wish I felt safest at home."

"I'm sure you could find another roommate if you post an ad on campus."

"Oh." Jenna feels the conversation shift out of the hypothetical. She nods her head slowly.

"I'm sorry to do this to you Jenna."

"It's okay. You need to take care of yourself right now." Jenna leans back into the soft cushions of the couch, her hands limp at her sides. "Don't worry about me."

Chapter Two

When Jenna sits down across from her college advisor, dropping her book bag at her feet and saying she's decided to drop out, Professor Reed stands up without saying a word. At first, Jenna thinks she's leaving the room.

Professor Reed shuts the door, something she's never done when Jenna has come to her office over the past three years. She doesn't speak until she's back sitting behind her desk. "How does your mother feel about this?" she asks.

Jenna sits in the oatmeal-colored chair with her arms crossed, holding her elbows. In their first advising meeting, Professor Reed told Jenna to call her by her first name. Unable to do this, Jenna tries never to address her. Behind Helen Reed's head, the sky outside the window is bright and makes her short, white hair look even whiter.

Her mother's opinion has hardly occurred to her. Jenna shrugs.

"She doesn't care you're dropping out of college?"

"I haven't told her." At this point, Jenna thinks, it isn't about how people feel.

Helen sits quietly with her hands folded under her chin. When Jenna took Philosophy 101 her first semester, it made her consider becoming a philosophy major. Helen forces her students to think for themselves, never revealing her own point of view. It's well known that Helen is in a long-term relationship with a woman and has two daughters from a previous marriage, but most of this has been pieced together from the stories of other students, the two framed pictures she displays in her office. There are rumors she was once a nun, but these could be false. Helen Reed never discusses her personal life.

"Have you considered hospice?"

Jenna grips her elbows tighter and shakes her head. Whenever the doctors say this word, her mother finds a way to change the subject.

Helen crosses her long legs. She's wearing a turtleneck, faded black jeans, and no makeup. Jenna has always wondered if she's the kind of feminist who doesn't shave her legs, but she always wears long black socks, even in May.

"And your sister?"

Jenna shakes her head, considering Julie's aversion to hospitals and responsibility. "There's no one else."

As a sophomore, when Jenna had to declare a major, she chose an integrated major focusing on sociology which allowed her to take a philosophy course every semester. And she was able to keep Helen as her advisor.

Helen leans back in her chair and sighs. "Let's call this a leave of absence," she says. "That way you won't lose all your money, and the paperwork will be easier when you decide to return."

Through the window, Jenna watches her classmates on the green lawn of her small campus. They sit on blankets in front of the library or hurry to class, probably worrying about papers addressing gender inequality and the drunken decisions they made on Friday night. Jenna envies their quaint, inconsequential troubles.

Helen opens a desk drawer and rifles through it.

"I don't know how long I'll be gone," Jenna says.

"That's okay. We'll stay in touch." Helen holds out a form and Jenna lets go of her elbows, leans forward in her chair, and reaches out.

***

Jenna doesn't post an ad for a new roommate. Instead, she fills her Camry with boxes, some of which were never unpacked, and drives back to Manchester. She knows she'll pay a penalty for breaking the lease, but she doesn't care. She'll call the landlord. Maybe she'll cry and get off easier. Surely it will be no trouble to re-rent the apartment.

Jenna doesn't tell anyone she's coming home, and by the time her mother returns from her current trip, there will be nothing to discuss. She gets back her job at Dunkin' Donuts, where she worked over the summer. It's the kind of job she can do without thinking or taking home with her. It's also a job that can be ditched at a moment's notice in an emergency.

Since the summer, the employees have gotten new uniforms. Jenna keeps her smock hanging in the back of her car. She washes off the powdered sugar and jelly at the end of each day and puts the smock on as she walks inside the building from the parking lot. The uniform is decidedly unflattering, especially on anyone beyond a size two. Jenna has curves. Her breasts are large and high, something of which she's always been somewhat proud. She figures this will change someday, and she'll grow envious of small-chested older women who can still go braless. But for now, she considers them an asset. She has come to accept her hips and ass, wider than the supposed ideal, but appealing in their own way. They fill a dress out quite nicely, punctuated by her shapely calves. The uniform, however, doesn't do her any favors. It's poop-brown with seaming right under her breasts. The resulting arch of fabric over her belly makes her look as if she's expecting. In her first week, three customers ask about her due date.

The first time it happens, Jenna flushes red and stammers. She gets more embarrassed than the stupid woman who asked.

There's no way to smooth out this sort of misunderstanding. The woman pays for her chocolate creams and leaves quickly.

The second time, Jenna gets pissed off. This time it's a man. "It's the smock!" she snaps. He nods, snatches his coffee off the counter, and nearly knocks down another customer on his way out the door.

The third time, Jenna beams. "March," she says.

"How nice." The white-haired woman is buying a box of munchkins. She wears a chunky beige sweater covered in fall leaves. "Do you know if it's a boy or a girl?"

"I've decided to be surprised," Jenna tells her.

The woman pulls out a dozen or so napkins from the dispenser, smiling. "Back when I had my kids, they weren't doing those tests, and we had no choice but to be surprised. I think it's better that way."

Jenna agrees.

***

Bill and Julie watch *The Price is Right* together in the den as Jenna gets ready for work. After the first surgery, Bill's brain went without oxygen for too long. As part of his recovery, the occupational therapist gave him homework, workbooks to help him remember things that were once a daily nuisance, like writing checks or how to figure out the tip at a restaurant. It seemed so tedious then, but Jenna misses it now. Now, there's no need.

Julie cries out in mock-anguish as the price of a can of tuna is revealed and her guess proves way off.

"You'd be better at this if you ever went grocery shopping," Jenna tells her.

. Julie sticks out her tongue. "I'll do the shopping if you let me borrow your car."

"I have to go to work." Jenna walks out to the kitchen and gets her oatmeal out of the microwave.

Julie follows her. "I'll drive you."

Jenna sits at the table and looks at her sister suspiciously. "What's wrong with your car?"

"Nothing. It does this thing sometimes. No big deal."

Jenna pauses with a spoonful of oatmeal halfway to her mouth. "You have no gas."

Julie huffs. "Come on Jenna," she whines.

"Fine. But I have to go in about three minutes."

"Cool."

"And you'll do the shopping?" Jenna holds out the list and Julie takes it.

"Yeah." She shoves it in her back pocket.

"But quickly. So, Bill isn't alone too long." Jenna says this quietly although there's no way Bill will hear.

"I know."

On the way to Dunkin's, Julie pulls into the post office.

"What the hell? I'm going to be late as it is!"

"I'll be a minute." Julie jumps out of the car, leaving it running, before Jenna can argue any further.

Angrily, Jenna flips the visor down and looks at her reflection in the narrow rectangle. The dark circles under her eyes might finally be fading. She has to admit she's been sleeping better since moving home. She hasn't heard from Liam since he left last week. His mother drove up to collect him and his things. She hugged Jenna and thanked her for keeping an eye on him. *Fat lot of good it seems to have done,* Jenna thinks.

It's not entirely true she hasn't heard from him. She did get a group email containing his mother's address. Jenna hasn't replied. She thinks about sending him a Get-Well card but isn't sure how those work for mental illness.

The driver's side door clicks open and Jenna's about to snap at her sister for being so slow when a man slides in next to her.

Jenna holds her breath. She has absolutely no impulse to save herself. Vaguely, she wonders about the whole fight or flight thing. She does neither. Just sits there as he shifts the car into reverse. She doesn't jump out of the car. Doesn't try to pull the keys out of the ignition or scratch out his eyes. She doesn't even scream.

The man turns to look out the back window as he backs up and that's when he sees her there beside him, sitting silent and wide-eyed.

"Holy shit!" The brakes squeak and the car rocks in place. "What are you doing in my car?"

Jenna swallows uncertainly. Where are her survival instincts? It's like the time she tripped and fell at a restaurant when she was thirteen and didn't put her hands out to stop her fall. She hit the hardwood floor with her face, sending up a wish to the heavens the impact would knock her out. No such luck. That tended to be the response Jenna got from the heavens. She landed face first and heard the thud of her face hitting the floor from an insider's perspective, an auditory experience no one else could've had.

He looks around. The backseat littered with women's clothing. Julie's pink CD case on the seat next to him. "Oh man." He closes his eyes and leans against the steering wheel. "I got in the wrong car." He laughs as he shifts the car into drive and returns to the parking space. He looks over at Jenna. "You okay? I'm sorry. Hey, did I scare you?"

When the danger is over and it's clear it was all a misunderstanding, this guy wasn't trying to hurt her, and she's safe—that's when Jenna starts to cry.

He starts stammering then, apologizing and explaining his car looks exactly like this one. It's parked nearby, and he can prove it. When Julie walks out of the building, she spots the two of them sitting in the car, and sees Jenna is crying. Before Jenna can warn either of them, Julie yanks open his door and starts screaming at him. She pulls him out of the car by the back of his jacket and in a combination of lost balance and surprise, he tumbles out onto the pavement with his hands up, covering his face as Julie fumbles in her purse for her mace.

Finally, Jenna manages to halt her blubbering and yell, "No, no, Julie. He didn't mean it."

Julie shifts her weight and squints down at him, still pointing her mace in his direction.

Jenna gets out and walks around the car. By now there are some passersby on the sidewalk, staring but not getting involved.

"It was an accident. Can you put away the mace?" he shouts from behind his hands.

Julie looks unconvinced.

"Can you tell her?" He looks up at Jenna in a panic.

"Julie, put away the mace. It was a misunderstanding." Jenna gives him her hand and he takes it. She pulls him up off the ground and he dusts off his pants.

"Misunderstanding?" Julie puts her mace away with reluctance. "Why are you crying then?"

"I'm not." Jenna feels her face redden.

"You were," she insists.

"I got into the wrong car and freaked her out," he tells Julie. He turns to Jenna. "Sorry about that. Are you okay?"

Jenna nods. "You?"

He looks down at his dirty pants and laughs. "I'm fine...I'm Sam." He holds out his hand and Jenna shakes it.

"Jenna."

"Nice to meet you?" he says uncertainly, laughing again. The corners of his eyes crinkle into starbursts.

Julie folds her arms across her chest. "Aren't you going to be late for work?" she says to Jenna.

"Where do you work?" Sam asks.

"Dunkin's."

Julie gets into the car and sticks her head out the window. "Be a little more careful whose car you get into, *Sam*."

"I sure will. Sorry again."

Jenna walks back to the passenger side of the car, lifting her hand in a sheepish goodbye before ducking inside.

Julie pauses before pulling onto the main road. In a voice that's quiet and small, she says, "You never cry."

"I'm fine," Jenna says. She can feel her sister's eyes on her. "Let's go."

***

Dunkin' Donuts is famous for claiming their donuts are made fresh every morning. Throughout the eighties and nineties, Jenna's entire childhood, television commercials featured a chubby, mustached man who woke before dawn, mumbling: "It's time to make the donuts. Time to make the donuts."

Jenna can't get his sluggish mantra out of her head as she walks into the building. Since the donut counter is located inside of a gas station convenience store, her duties don't include making the donuts. A delivery truck arrives early in the morning with donuts on huge metal cooling racks. Jenna witnessed this several times over the summer. The truck arrives at two a.m., after the workers have thrown out all the donuts that haven't been sold. Dozens, sometimes hundreds, of donuts are tossed into the giant blue dumpster behind the store.

It's sad, really, the waste. Jelly-filled and chocolate-glazed and rainbow sprinkles turned to rubbish in the twilight of a parking lot. Jenna prefers the day shift.

The bells on the front door jingle as Jenna steps behind the counter and puts on her headset.

"Hey, Jimmy," she says.

Jimmy doesn't answer. He watches Jenna like she's a gazelle in the Serengeti and he's afraid of spooking her. He's wearing bike shorts, and a Polaroid camera hangs around his neck. He lifts the camera to his face, presses a button, and the flash goes off. He leaves before the picture has time to develop.

"Doesn't that bother you?" her coworker Ashley asks.

"Who, Jimmy?" Jenna points out the door. "He's harmless."

"Molly says he puts those pictures up behind the counter at the bike shop."

"Really?"

Ashley nods. "He calls you the donut girl."

"Huh." Jimmy works across the street. Jenna got used to the photo routine over the summer. "That's actually kind of funny."

Ashley shakes her head. "I think I'd get a restraining order."

Jenna laughs at this.

"He's crazy Jenna," Ashley insists.

Jenna shrugs. "He's a weird kid." Jenna isn't fazed by people's eccentricities. Everyone is a little bit crazy. It's all about degrees. In Liam's graduating class, there was a girl who wore a T-shirt and a pair of Depends underneath her graduation robe. Still, she got her diploma designating her as a meaningful contributor to society. Then there was the man who drove in from Lowell to get his iced coffee made by Jenna. He wasn't hitting on her; it wasn't about that. He became genuinely flustered when she wasn't working and had to be convinced to give another coffee maker a try. The convenience store owner's son had a condition called Trichotillomania, which made him pull out his hair when he got stressed out. Jenna saw him do it once when he was stocking shelves and thought he was alone. It was somewhat frightening, but otherwise he came across as a regular guy. And Ashley had no right to judge, as far as Jenna was concerned. Weighing hardly one-hundred pounds, she ogled the donuts all day and never ate one.

At the end of Jenna's shift, Julie is nowhere to be seen. A computer voice answers Julie's cell, suggesting she hasn't paid the bill, and no one answers when Jenna calls home. She gets a ride from a coworker and tries not to panic, taking the front steps two at a time.

"Bill?" she calls out to him from the hall. The prospect of waking him from a nap is the least of her worries.

He's there, sitting in his blue chair. "I have to go to the bathroom," he says, without a greeting.

Jenna helps him to his feet, and they walk down the hall together. She waits for him outside the bathroom, grateful for elastic waistbands. Leaning against the wall, she can see into the den. On the table beside his chair she sees his breakfast dishes, his empty juice glass.

Walking him back to his chair, she tries to keep her voice even. "Julie hasn't been home all day?"

"Nope."

"I'll go make you something to eat."

Bill stops her. He puts a hand on the side of her face and smiles right into her soul. "My sweet girl."

In the kitchen, Jenna makes him a fluffernutter as Norman drools at her feet. The smell of peanut butter is about the only thing that can lure him away from Bill. When the girls were little, Bill used to make them fluffernutters on weekends. It was probably the easiest thing he knew how to make, unaccustomed to the finicky appetites of children, but to Jenna and Julie it always felt like a special occasion.

Jenna cuts the crusts off out of habit. She tosses the knife into the sink and puts the peanut butter and marshmallow fluff back into the pantry. She brings a ginger ale and opens it with a quick snap and hiss before he can ask.

"To tide you over," she says as he takes the plate from her. "I'll make dinner in a while."

He nods at her with his mouth full. "Sit with me," he urges her, and she's reminded that beyond his basic physical needs, he's also lonely.

She sits on the couch beside him. Norman lies on the floor between them, his snout between his paws, paying close attention to every bite Bill takes. Officially, he isn't begging. Begging's not allowed. Jenna isn't quite sure about the criteria.

"There's nothing on," Bill says, holding the remote out to her.

"That's okay." She waves a hand to indicate refusal.

"Take it," he insists, as if it's all he has to offer.

Jenna takes the remote and flips channels idly. She pauses on a casting episode for the new season of a reality show. Due to his poor hearing, Bill watches television with the captions on. A southern boy, talking about his family says, "My father's a simple good old boy and my mother's a pretty little doll."

The captions say, "My father's a simple little doll."

Bill laughs. "This show must be funnier to the deaf."

After he finishes his sandwich, Bill dozes. Jenna lowers the volume on the television. She remembers the day all those years ago when she ran in from the backyard to find Julie sitting on his lap, giggling at a joke. Their mother sat beside him, beaming. They made such a pretty picture. Jenna was livid. She glared at her sister, whose laughter caught in her throat, like the traitor she knew she was. Jenna ran upstairs, flung herself on her bed and sobbed.

Their joint assault fell apart quickly after that, and it was the last time they were ever truly on the same page.

Norman pushes his head under her hand to request a pat. Jenna marvels at this direct, unabashed statement of need.

***

After dinner, Julie slinks into the house. She has her head bent, looking like Norman after he pees on the rug.

Jenna's sitting at the kitchen table, facing the door. Waiting for her. Bill used to sit like this whenever the girls went out on dates. Once when Jenna got home late, his deep voice boomed, "Tell me you were in an accident." Jenna wasn't allowed to go out with that boy ever again, which was probably for the best. He had trouble written all over him.

"Tell me you were in an accident," Jenna says now.

Julie jumps. "Jenna."

"Were you in an accident?" she asks louder.

Julie sighs. "No."

"Where are the groceries?"

Julie winces, as if this might have saved her.

"Bill was alone all day," Jenna says.

"I'm sorry." Julie collapses into the chair across from Jenna.

"Sorry? He nearly pissed himself!"

Julie covers her face and starts to cry.

"What is the matter with you?" Jenna hisses.

"I got in a fight with Brad."

"Brad?"

"My *boy*friend!" In the midst of everything, she manages to sound a little offended Jenna doesn't know his name.

"Oh, well, this explains everything." Jenna leans back into her chair, hugging her body to contain the shaking. She never feels this kind of rage at anyone else in her life. Just Julie.

"It was awful." Julie's still crying.

"Do you really think we're going to sit here and talk about your fight with your boyfriend?" Jenna leans across the table. She wants to rip Julie's hair out in clumps. "Boo. Hoo. Find someone who gives a shit."

There is a high-pitched cluck in the back of Julie's throat. Then her wide-eyed expression crumbles, and she runs up the stairs.

Jenna waits until she can control her breathing before returning to the den.

***

"I'll take two honey-glazed and your Toyota Camry."

Jenna looks up from the register.

"Pretty please," he adds.

"Sam!"

"You remember my name." He smiles and there are those starbursts.

"Of course. It isn't every day I get almost-car-jacked."

"Well, that's good to hear. That would be stressful if it happened every day."

Jenna tips her head at him and laughs.

"Do you have any idea how many Dunkin' Donuts there are in Manchester?"

"I do. They pretty much drill it into us during training."

"So, tell me." He leans in, conspiratorially.

"Fifty-four," Jenna whispers.

"Whoa. That's a lot of donuts."

Jenna nods. "Speaking of. Two glazed, you said?"

"Well, what would you recommend? Speaking as an expert."

"Oh, well, as an expert." Jenna smiles. "I like the honey-glazed best, myself."

"Okay, two then."

Jenna shakes open a paper bag.

"If you have a break soon, one of those could be yours."

"I don't. I already took my break."

"Ah." Sam shakes his head. He looks disappointed.

Jenna remembers what he said earlier. "You were looking for me? For what?"

Sam clears his throat. "I needed a donut expert?" He shakes his head. "No, I guess I wanted to see you again."

"Oh." It dawns on Jenna slowly. She slides his donuts into the bag and smiles with her back turned.

"To apologize again," he adds, quickly.

Jenna's smile fades as she turns to the cash register. "Oh." She sets his bag on the counter.

"Over dinner?"

Sam leaves with his donuts and Jenna's phone number.

"Is he the father?"

Jenna turns to look at Molly, the coworker whose existence she has forgotten. "Father?"

Molly nods. "Ashley overheard you tell a customer you were pregnant."

"Oh. No. No, he's a friend." Jenna presses her lips together. *This isn't happening,* she tells herself. Sometimes she pretends she's an actor in a play. It's easier to do around people who don't really know her. Which is everyone.

"Are you okay?"

Jenna realizes she's leaning against the counter with her eyes closed.

"Why don't you sit down out back?"

***

Her mother sits on the edge of her bed. Jenna's eyes flutter open and search for the clock. It's after midnight.

"Julie told me you were home." Barbara whispers.

"I'm taking a leave of absence," Jenna says quickly, anticipating the need for a defense.

"It's freezing in here." Barbara stands to close the window. At night, Jenna likes to leave it open a crack in all but the coldest weather. She burrows under the pile of blankets, warm except for the tip of her nose.

The window thumps against the sill and Barbara stands quietly, looking out at the dark street below.

Jenna sits up in bed. "Mom?"

Barbara continues to look out the window. "This might surprise you, but I'm not going to argue with you. You're old enough to make your own decisions."

Oddly, Jenna feels disappointed.

No one from school has called to ask what happened to her. She can imagine someone noticing, making her a topic of conversation, a mystery that would go unsolved as another campus drama stole focus.

Barbara turns around, rubbing the chill from her arms. "The truth is we need you here right now." She walks to the door, the light from the hall turning her into a silhouette. "School will always be there later."

Jenna can only nod. These are points she planned on making.

"Welcome home." Barbara pulls the door closed firmly behind her.

Chapter Three

Late on Friday night, after being home for over a week, Jenna checks her email. She has one from Liam, a single line, no greeting. He doesn't type his name at the end. It reads:

"I feel like you've abandoned me."

The house is dark and quiet. Bill has been asleep for hours. No one else is home. Jenna leans back in the computer chair, pressing her palms against the smooth wooden surface of the desk. Circling the drain of his bottomless need, she reminds herself Liam hasn't always been this way.

Jenna met Liam when he was the Resident Advisor in her freshman dorm, organizing the get-to-know-you activities. He posted notices in the bathrooms on the inside of the stall doors so they could be read from the toilet. Everyone sat cross-legged in a circle as he passed around a bowl of Skittles. (M&M's would have worked too, but they melt faster, despite what they said in their old slogan.) For each Skittle taken, you told the group something about yourself. The questions were color-coded. A yellow Skittle was about your family; green was for your favorite subject in school.

By the third dorm meeting, everyone on the floor decided they knew each other well enough. Jenna was the only one to show up. Liam kept looking at his watch and turning deeper shades of red. She insisted they play Twister, and they did a decent job eating snacks intended for twenty people. By the end of the night, Liam shared his secret stash of wine coolers (a huge violation of RA code), and they fell asleep on the floor in his room.

Liam was the only one of Jenna's friends who knew Bill was sick. He was the only person she talked to about anything serious in her life. He never judged her or tried to tell her what to do. She always thought these were signs of a good listener, of unconditional acceptance. Now, she wonders if he doesn't care about things that don't affect him. Maybe her world outside of him simply doesn't matter.

She stares at Liam's email, reading it over and over to herself in different tones. Is it a joke? Sarcasm? She reads the line so many times that the words dissolve before her eyes and become meaningless.

Jenna signs off and goes to bed.

***

Sam's Camry does in fact look exactly like Jenna's. Black exterior, gray cloth seats. Inside, it's tidier. But maybe he cleaned in preparation for their date.

The car radio plays "Tupelo Honey." Sam listens to the same station Jenna does. It's the only one in the area that plays Ani DiFranco.

"I love this part," he tells her, tapping the beat on the steering wheel. "The way he says it, 'All the tea in *Chinay*.' Don't you love Van Morrison?"

He turns to her, grinning. She hesitates, wanting to give an honest answer. She hasn't given her feelings for Van Morrison much thought before this.

"Sorry. I talk a lot when I'm nervous," he says. "What kind of music do you like?"

He's nervous? Jenna thinks.

At dinner, Sam looks at her over the top of the menu. "Does your sister still want to mace me?"

Jenna laughs. "Our dad gave it to her a few years ago, and she's been itching for the chance to use it ever since."

"Does she know you're out with me?"

Jenna shakes her head.

Sam nods slowly.

"It's not like a secret or anything. It's just." She wants to keep him from taking it personally, but she also wants to avoid revealing too much. "We're not exactly talking to each other right now." She shrugs, and Sam doesn't pry.

She orders the pasta; he gets a hamburger and fries. They talk about their childhoods and bond over having parents who divorced when they were four and remarried when they were six. Unlike Jenna, Sam's mother divorced a second time, after adopting a little girl from Korea.

"For weeks, I went to school bragging *my* baby sister was coming on an airplane. Everyone else had little brothers and sisters who came out of their moms. *Boring*."

He talks with his hands and makes funny faces. Jenna pushes her bangs out of her eyes.

"When I finally met her for the first time, Tara was eighteen months old. I showed her my best break-dancing moves at the gate in the airport. She was unimpressed." He shrugs. "I told my parents she wasn't as cool as I'd expected."

Jenna laughs. The waitress arrives with their food and they both lean back as she sets their plates in front of them. There's a pause in the natural flow of conversation which persists for a while after the waitress leaves. Jenna slides the ketchup across the table. "Did your family learn Korean?"

Sam thanks her and starts arranging the order of toppings on his burger. He removes every other ring in the white onion and sets the lettuce leaf aside completely. He makes a triangle out of the three small pickles, circles touching but not overlapping. "My mother tried for a little while. Just some basic words when she first got here." He squeezes ketchup on the bun, pressing the slice of tomato into the condiment and fitting the two halves of the burger together. "But it didn't last long. Tara picked up English quickly, which was probably easier than waiting for us to learn Korean."

"Korean must be difficult. I don't know if I could learn a whole new alphabet."

Sam nods. "I've lost all my high school French. Now, all I can say is *ferme la porte, s'il vous plait.*"

"Which means?"

"Shut the door, please. I can also tell you my name and ask where the library is. Extremely useful."

"Better than what I remember from my sign language class." Jenna holds up her index finger. "One sign."

Sam sets his burger back on his plate, giving her his full attention.

"It's not polite," Jenna warns.

"Well, be quiet then."

Jenna's hand sweeps down toward her abdomen, the womb. Her hand grasps something invisible in a scooping motion and then moves quickly away from the body to discard its imaginary contents.

"What is it?" Sam asks.

"Abortion."

"No sugar coating with that one."

"Nope." Jenna looks around the restaurant self-consciously, hoping no one has understood what she's said or taken it out of context.

"Are deaf people blunter in general?"

"I don't know. I don't know any deaf people."

"Why did you want to learn sign language?"

Jenna hesitates, trying to imagine how the truth might sound. She doesn't want him to think she's weird. "I wanted to be able to talk to gorillas."

"Gorillas?"

"Yeah. Remember Koko, the gorilla? She learned sign language and asked for a cat?"

Sam nods.

Jenna shrugs. "I've always wanted to have a conversation with a gorilla. But I couldn't hold onto the language."

"It's harder as we age. Kids pick up languages faster."

"Does your sister still speak Korean?"

Sam frowns. "I guess she didn't have anyone Korean to talk to."

"How old is she now?" Jenna twirls her fork in the mass of linguine.

"Nineteen. She's in college in Florida."

Jenna sets down her fork. "How old are you?"

"Twenty-six." He smiles. "Is this a problem?"

Jenna reaches for her soda. "No."

"How old are you?"

Jenna swallows. "Twenty-one. Is *that* a problem?"

Sam shakes his head. "Not at all."

He talks about moving to Manchester when he was thirteen, about growing up in Chicago. She tells him her brother is in medical school there.

"Your mother must be proud."

"I guess so." The truth is, Jenna has never overheard her mother boasting about any of her children.

When he asks if she's in college, she wants to change the subject. She isn't sure why. "Doesn't Dunkin' Donuts employee say it all?"

"Not necessarily."

"Well, I was in college. I had to take a leave recently. Um." She struggles with the right way to say it. "Family illness."

"Oh. Sorry to hear that." Again, Sam seems to sense he shouldn't delve further. "What was your major?"

"Sociology."

"Cool." He stuffs a few fries into his mouth.

"What do you do?" As she asks, she wonders why it took so long to get here. *Isn't this where most conversations start?*

He sums up his job as a loan processor in a single sentence and quickly moves the conversation back to things he seems to find more interesting. They talk more about family, how he worries about his sister living on her own far away. There's nearly the same age difference between Jenna and Billy. They argue about the advantages and disadvantages of being an older brother versus a younger sister. Sam believes parents are harder on first born sons; they must set an example. Jenna disagrees completely. Daughters are unfairly overprotected and kept from experiencing life as fully.

"And your sister? Are you twins?"

Jenna looks across the table, incredulous. "How did you know that?"

Sam shrugs. "I don't know. Just a guess."

"No one ever guesses that."

"Maybe it was how fiercely she protected you. That whole twin-bond thing. She wanted to *murder* me." His thick eyebrows jump and dive toward each other.

Jenna laughs. "That's not the twin thing. That's Julie."

When the check comes, Jenna pulls out her wallet. Sam waves her off. "You can pay next time," he says.

Next time.

Jenna smiles as she slips her wallet into her purse. "Well, thanks."

He shrugs. "Don't thank me yet. I may order the lobster."

"Ah. I'll consider myself warned."

When they get to her house, he asks if he can walk her to her door.

"Oh, that's okay." As she says it, she wonders if she has ruined the chances of a goodnight kiss. It's been a while since she's been on a proper date, and she's forgotten the protocol.

"Is anyone home?" Sam asks. Besides the flickering porch light, the house is dark.

"My dad."

"Is he the one who's...sick?"

Jenna nods, staring at her lap. "His heart is—" She turns to Sam. "He's dying." She's never said it aloud before and as the words leave her mouth, she finds herself unable to take another breath. She opens her eyes wider as they fill, horrifyingly, with tears. She thinks if she can keep the tears from overflowing, they'll both be able to pretend this isn't happening.

She feels a tear escape, sliding slowly down the side of her nose. As she's wondering whether it's too dark inside the car for him to see her, Sam opens the center console and retrieves a napkin. He holds it out to her, and she presses it to her face and turns away from him.

"I'm sorry," he says.

She shrugs, squeezing her eyes shut to keep the rest of the tears from coming. Dimly, she can see her reflection in the glass of the passenger window. She wants to avoid the puffy splotches, the inevitable result of any good cry. She has never been a pretty crier. "It's not your fault."

He's quiet for a moment, as if mulling this over. "Well, still," he says.

Jenna turns back toward him, forcing a smile. "I'm not usually like this."

"It's okay."

"You probably think I cry all the time since that's what I seem to do when I'm with you. But I don't."

He shakes his head. "I don't think that. You seem tough." He motions to her lap where she holds the shredded paper napkin between clenched fists.

Jenna allows a small laugh.

"Maybe you feel comfortable with me," he suggests.

"Lucky you." She looks up. He smiles at her, so she smiles back.

Sam reaches for her hand and squeezes it. "Let me walk you to your door."

He kisses her there, under the porch light, right on the mouth. She holds her breath, and it all happens in slow motion. "I can't wait to see you again," he says and despite her nature, she believes him.

****

Bill Jr. and Annie bring Lucas over on Sunday.

Lucas is five and has his daddy's ice-blue eyes, the ones that also match his grandfather's perfectly. The three of them look like a freakish exercise in cloning. When Jenna first met Bill's son, six years ago when they returned to the states, the two men looked like brothers. You might have guessed they were only a handful of years apart.

Annie was newly pregnant then. For over a decade, the two of them traveled around the world like nomads. They couldn't attend his father's wedding because they were in Bangladesh. Jenna remembers her fascination with the word at the time. It sounded like the most exotic, faraway place she could imagine.

Since then, they'd been to Morocco, Ireland, Amsterdam. Jenna was always fuzzy about the details of what exactly they did in these places. Being there was enough explanation. All of that came to an end when Annie got pregnant. Jenna isn't sure which of them insisted on it. They still live an unconventional life—Annie working as a cook at the vegan co-op, Bill Jr. teaching at the school there—but they've been in the same tiny community in Vermont for six years now.

Annie crouches down and whispers to Lucas at the door to the den. "Be gentle with Grampa. He's still not feeling well."

Lucas nods, wide-eyed and serious. Jenna isn't sure what his parents have told him or how much he can be expected to understand. He watches as his father enters the room.

"It's good to see you, Dad," Bill Jr. says. He gives a single, gentle handshake.

Bill divorced his mother when he was quite young and was mostly absent during his childhood. Still, Bill Jr. calls him Dad. Jenna and Julie have lived in his house for fifteen years, nearly their entire lives, but have always called him Bill. This is backward to Jenna, who feels more like Bill's daughter than she has the right to.

"Lucas!" Bill lights up. Deep in his gray haggard face, those ice-blue eyes shine.

Tentatively, Lucas touches his grandfather's knee. Bill tussles the boy's sandy hair.

"Show Grampa the present you made," Annie prompts, sitting on the far side of the couch beside her husband.

Lucas reaches into his pocket and pulls out an elastic bracelet strung with beads of differing colors and shapes.

"You made this for me?" Bill takes it and holds it closer to his face. "It's great. Thank you so much."

Lucas pulls his sleeve up and holds out his own wrist. "I have one too!"

After some fumbling, Bill manages to get the bracelet on. He leans forward and holds his wrist out for everyone to appraise.

"It's beautiful, Lucas!" Jenna says. "I can't believe you made that all by yourself."

Lucas' expression falls. "I'll make you one next time."

Jenna laughs. "Don't worry about it, kiddo. You don't have to bring presents for everyone."

Lucas smiles uncertainly. He's hypersensitive to every little shift in the emotional atmosphere. Jenna wonders if he remembers when Bill was well. Two years ago, when Lucas was three, Bill wrestled on the floor with him, gave him piggy-back rides, and blew raspberries on his tummy. Now, Bill lacks the strength to lift his grandson onto his lap.

"Lucas wants to make jewelry when he grows up," Annie informs everyone.

"No, Mother." Lucas rolls his eyes. "Just bracelets. The other stuff is too hard."

"He's going to specialize," Bill Jr. laughs.

"And necklaces," Lucas adds after thinking.

"Wow, that's great." Bill nods and Jenna wonders if he's really following the conversation.

Lucas pulls himself onto his father's lap, and Bill Jr. holds one leg out straight. Lucas shimmies out onto it, grinning before the ride starts. Bill Jr. shakes his leg gently at first, then in jerks matching the boy's bursts of laughter. Jenna sits on the floor with Norman as Annie talks about the surprise zucchini she found growing in their compost pile. Bill Jr.'s leg becomes a bucking bronco, and Lucas is tossed to the floor in a fit of giggles.

Annie recites a recipe for pumpkin soup Jenna pretends to pay attention to. It sounds good, but Jenna doesn't cook anything with more than three ingredients. While they lived together, she and Liam took turns making dinner. He made frittatas and vegetarian lasagna and meatloaf. She made bacon cheeseburgers, tuna steaks with rice noodles, and spaghetti with sauce from the can.

They lower their voices as Bill's head lolls and snaps back to attention several times.

When he falls asleep, they go into the backyard. Lucas tries to play with Norman, who has grown too old to find children interesting. Lucas throws a stick three times before he gives up.

He sits in the grass, patting Norman and telling him long stories Jenna strains to hear.

"What's he saying?" She sits on the back steps with Annie and Bill Jr.

"Who knows?" Annie says, smiling. "He has a very rich fantasy world."

Lucas flops beside Norman in the grass, laughing.

"He's sweet," Jenna says.

"Thanks," Bill Jr. says. "We like him." He sits on the step behind Annie, running his fingers through her dark, somewhat tangled hair. Jenna remembers when Annie had dreadlocks, followed by a look that was so short she was nearly bald. She had the bone structure to make it look almost regal. Now, Annie's hair falls to the middle of her back.

"How is your mother holding up?" Annie asks.

Jenna lets out her breath slowly. "Okay, I guess."

Bill Jr. and Annie nod in unison as if they know this is impossible.

"Where's Julie?"

"I'm not sure. We keep missing each other. Partially by design." Jenna blows her hair out of her eyes. "We're taking turns being home." She's surprised at the sunny picture she's able to whip up at a moment's notice.

"So, you've left school?" Bill Jr. asks.

"Yeah. I couldn't stand not being here right now."

"You better go back."

"I will."

"Bill was so proud of you," he says, and she hears the past tense. "Did you know that?"

Lucas rolls onto his belly and tucks his legs underneath him, bottom in the air, making the up-down-up shape of an inch worm.

Jenna smiles even though it hurts.

***

The first time Liam calls, Jenna doesn't answer. She isn't exactly sure why, but it tires her to imagine the argument he wants to have about what a bad friend she's been lately. He doesn't leave a message.

The only thing they ever argued about was Jenna's tendency to play devil's advocate, or as Liam called it: her attempt to see the world from every possible point of view. Liam used to get annoyed when he saw the campus groundskeepers playing touch football on the lawn out their window.

"Our tuition is paying for that," he'd say, glaring out the window.

"Maybe it's their lunch break," Jenna would suggest.

"Every time I see them, they're goofing off."

"Maybe it only seems like that."

One day, Liam groaned. "Why can't you ever take *my* side?"

The second time he calls, she excuses herself from the den where Bill has fallen asleep watching *Wheel of Fortune*.

"Hello?"

"Jenna, what happened to you?"

It's an interesting question, Jenna thinks. One that could take years to answer. "What do you mean?" she says instead.

"I haven't heard from you in two weeks."

Jenna sits on the living room couch without turning the light on. "I know. I've been busy. I moved home."

"You did?" He pauses. "I'm going a little crazy at *my* house. My mother is always here. Always asking if she can make me something to eat. I know she means well, but you know how moms can be."

"Yeah," Jenna murmurs, but she has no idea. Her mother has never been the over- involved, suffocating type. Growing up, it always seemed like Jenna's mother was the one who felt suffocated.

"I started taking the Zoloft."

"Is that helping?"

"Takes a few weeks to kick in. Right now, my head feels weird. Like my brain gets hot and cold, buzzing."

"I think I'd heard that can happen."

"Did you get my email?" he asks, finally.

"Yep."

"And you didn't reply?"

"I wasn't sure what to say. I mean, were you serious?"

"Serious?"

"You feel like I abandoned you?"

"Yes, Jenna."

"Well, that seems really unfair."

"Well, I'm sorry. It's how I feel, and a feeling isn't right or wrong."

Jenna is quiet, thinking about this.

"You don't call," Liam continues. "You don't write. You don't ask how I am. What am I supposed to think?"

"I'm busy."

"Doing what?"

"My dad is sick, Liam. Remember?"

"Your dad is always sick."

It feels like a million tiny pinpricks all the way up her body. *Yeah. And when's the last time you asked how I was doing?* But she doesn't say that. She hangs up.

There was a time when Liam was the only person who knew how she was doing. She could tell him anything, including the mean thoughts you're not supposed to admit having. In college, they took turns lying on the lumpy couch in his oversized, single dorm room. One of them would ramble on in a stream of consciousness while the other listened. It was their first experiment with talk therapy, without the benefit of a trained professional.

After each of them exhausted their words, Liam would hook up his Sega and beat Jenna at *Ultimate Fighting*. He played more than she did and knew the secret key combinations for all the complicated, winning moves. His player would do cartwheels and slam her player to the ground, and he pretended he didn't know how it happened. Whenever Jenna asked to be taught the trick, he looked at his controller as if it had a mind of its own.

Jenna marches into the den and startles Bill awake. "Sorry," she says, collecting his plates from dinner. "I'm going to clean up in the kitchen for a little while and then I'll be back to help you get ready for bed."

"Where's Barb?"

"Working late again."

"I want to wait up for her," he says uncertainly, like a child protesting his bedtime.

Jenna sighs. She hates the way he assumes she is in charge of him. But isn't she? "Okay," she says, letting him have his way and wishing she didn't have that power.

Chapter Four

Sam calls Monday evening, two days after their first date. Jenna's kneeling on the floor of her bedroom, digging through the container of shoes she keeps under her bed. Seeing his number on caller ID makes her feel ill.

She holds the phone, letting it ring again, weighing her options.

She says hello, and he says her name. She's read about the psychological appeal of hearing your name spoken by another person. Knowing this doesn't keep her from feeling it.

"That's me." She cradles the phone between her ear and shoulder, keeping her hands free for searching.

"How are you?" he asks.

"Fine. I'm fine." It's her mantra. She doesn't stop to think about it, focusing on the matter at hand: finding the mate for her brown clog.

"Say it enough and maybe someone will believe you."

She pauses, holding the first shoe in her lap. "Just not you?" She looks back into the bin. Each time she pulls something from the pile, it's another flip flop. She has a pair in every color to match whatever outfit she happens to wear. This way is easier, saves time. But as the first days of October announce themselves in red and yellow maple leaves and occasional morning windshield frost, it's getting too cold to wear flip flops.

"Nope," he says, and she can hear him grinning, imagines those creases in his face.

Jenna finds the other shoe at the bottom of the pile. She closes the container and slides it back under the bed.

They go over their schedules and decide they're both free the following night. She tells him she's determined not to cry this time. He laughs and tells her he has the perfect thing to do, but he won't tell her what it is.

"Can I come to the door, or should I wait in the driveway?"

"If you come to the door, my dad will want to meet you."

"Okay with me. If you think he's up to it."

Jenna's not expecting this. "Okay then." She wonders which version of her father Sam is going to meet.

***

It starts as pleasant little butterflies as she gets dressed to go out. She ends up stealing shoes from Julie's closet. Nothing ridiculous, a pair of black boots with a chunky, reasonable heel. They're sexy, the way they zip up the inside of her calf, stopping below the knee. But this is covered by her pant leg; it's a secret only she knows about.

By the time Sam's standing in the den, looking totally at ease making chit chat with Bill, Jenna feels downright queasy.

"Where you off to?" Bill leans forward, gripping the arms of his chair. The energy it takes to hold his body upright causes him to shake. Jenna wonders at this apparent display of masculinity for Sam's benefit. She wishes he would sit back.

"He won't tell me," she says. Sam shrugs.

Bill nods his approval. "I used to plan surprises for Jenna's mother."

The comparison makes her face flush.

As they turn to go, Bill winks at her. She sees a glimpse of him as he used to be.

Sam takes her to the arcade. As long as she's playing *Whack-a-Mole*, she's free of nervousness. Yellow tickets shoot out of the machine every time she lowers the hammer.

"I don't get it," he says. "Why are little raisins with faces popping out of the ground?"

"They're *moles*!" she laughs.

He bends to look at them closer. "Ah."

They don't talk much. The arcade is loud. They play racecar games, coming in behind all the other drivers, preoccupied with running each other off the road. When Jenna's car explodes in a cloud of fire and smoke, she shrieks, and when his explodes, she squeals. They laugh.

They carry armfuls of yellow tickets to the prize counter and lay them on top of the glass case.

Sam points to the fuzzy dice. "We should each get a different color so we can tell our cars apart."

Jenna makes a face. "Why don't *you* get a pair and that will make *your* car different?"

"You don't want to be tacky with me?"

Jenna gets the standard black and white dice; Sam gets a neon yellow pair. They leave the arcade, and he takes her hand. The queasiness returns.

He opens the car door for her. When he gets inside, he hangs his dice from the rearview mirror. "Nice, eh?"

Jenna shakes her head and smiles.

He leans in to kiss her quickly. "Where to next?" he asks. The sun is setting.

Jenna shrugs, still reeling from the kiss.

"Hungry?"

She nods.

"Okay. I know a place."

He takes them to a little diner downtown. Jenna misses the volume of the arcade, loud enough to shut out her own thoughts.

The diner has plastic menus big enough to hide behind. They sit across from each other in a red vinyl booth, talking about food and the time Sam met Adam Sandler here. They place their orders, and the waitress takes their menus, leaving nothing between them. Jenna fidgets.

Sam leans forward, elbows on the table. "How's your dad?"

"He's okay," she says, leaning back, wrapping both hands around her glass of ice water. "He's been doing a little better this week, I think." She wonders if she sounds too hopeful, like a person in deep denial. She tries to imagine him through Sam's eyes. "He has good days and bad days. You caught him on one of his better days."

Sam nods. "I'm glad."

"How did he seem to you?" She tries to ask this casually, as if his answer doesn't really matter.

"He seems like he loves you a lot."

She sighs. It isn't the answer she was looking for.

When Sam reaches for her hand, her pulse speeds up. "I could tell he was sick, but he seemed like a nice guy. Funny. And I think he likes me."

He grins at her and the lines around his eyes deepen and spread over his cheekbones, traveling down the sides of his face from his temples. They make her think of the streamers that come out of the handlebars of your very first bike. The kind with the basket and a banana seat. They say something about him, about his capacity for genuine happiness. And they're *beautiful*. Jenna knows she can't tell him that though; it would sound like she was making fun of him for having wrinkles. But Jenna thinks she could fall in love with him for those grooves in his face. Not only that. There are plenty of other reasons. But that's one.

Jenna pulls her hand away to rummage in her purse and pulls out her cell phone. "This is my nephew, Lucas." She holds the phone out to him, and he takes it. "Cute, huh?"

Sam nods. "He looks like you."

This makes her laugh. "We're not actually related. He's my stepbrother's kid."

Sam frowns, leaning in for a closer look. "Huh. Well, you're still both cute."

Jenna blushes. She puts her phone away. "He was visiting this weekend. He's five and so smart. We watched the penguin documentary together. He was glued to it."

"I saw that one. About how penguins mate and care for their babies?"

"Yeah."

"Penguins have it all figured out. Their year-long monogamy, getting to fall in love over and over throughout their lives. They're always in the fun part. They get to experience the butterflies forever."

Jenna tips her head, scrunches her face. "You think penguins get butterflies?"

"Why not?"

The waitress comes with their milkshakes.

"I actually think that sounds terrible," Jenna admits after the waitress leaves again.

"Why?"

"I hate the butterfly stage." She tears the paper wrapper of her straw and pounds her fist on the table, twice, releasing it.

"You do?"

Jenna groans. "Yeah. Maybe my butterflies are bigger than other peoples' but being around you pretty much makes me perpetually nauseous."

Sam raises his eyebrows. He looks startled, but also amused.

"No offense."

At the end of the night, he walks her to the door again. She feels breathless and disoriented under the flickering porch light, waiting for him to kiss her. Beyond the buzz of the dying lightbulb, she can hear the muffled sounds of Bill yelling.

She bolts into the house, Sam following her, but she holds out a hand like a traffic guard. "Stay," she says firmly in the voice she uses on Norman.

"Goddamn it! Goddamn it! Goddamn it!" Bill shouts, spittle flying from his lips.

She comes to a sudden stop in the doorway watching him. "What's wrong?"

"The flies are fornicating!" He aimlessly swings a rolled-up newspaper. Norman is up and wagging his tail at the excitement.

"What?"

"Right there!" he insists, finally landing a *thwack* against the arm of the couch. "See?"

Jenna doesn't see anything.

"Sonofabitch!" Bill struggles to get out of his chair, and Jenna tries to stop him. It's ridiculously easy. It reminds her of her futile attempts to strike out at Billy when she was younger. So much bigger and older, he used to press a hand against her forehead, and she could never make contact. She pushes gently on Bill's shoulders now, and he falls back into his chair.

To her horror, he starts to cry. "Get them. You have to get them."

Jenna looks around the room. "Where did they go, Bill?"

Bill rubs his eyes and leans forward. "There. On the windowsill," he says with confidence.

Jenna pulls a tissue out of the box on the coffee table and presses it against the windowsill. She balls it up and looks over her shoulder.

"Ha!" Bill claps.

Jenna starts out the door.

"Let me see."

Jenna pauses in the doorway. "No, I'm going to throw it away." She starts to leave again.

"Show me!"

Sighing, she walks toward him, opening the empty tissue in her palm.

Bill blinks a few times, then smiles. "Damn fornicators!"

Jenna closes her hand and leaves the room. She's surprised to find Sam waiting for her in the kitchen, leaning against the counter.

She tosses the Kleenex on the table.

"Is he okay?"

Not trusting her voice, Jenna shakes her head.

He touches her then, softly, right above the elbow of her left arm. "Can I do something to help?"

She pushes past him out the screen door and catches the railing of the porch. Pulling the cool night air into her lungs, she's determined to hold it together.

"You should go," she says when she hears him open the door behind her. It's easier to say without looking at him. "I'm sorry."

He's quiet at first. "If that's what you want."

She turns, nodding her head, not quite looking him in the eye.

He walks down the steps. "Call me?"

She tries to remember where her mother is tonight. Buffalo? It doesn't really matter. The number for her cell phone will be the same.

"Goodnight," she manages to say before disappearing inside the house.

***

Jenna's mother is due home that night. She arrives on the last flight into the tiny Manchester airport and meets Jenna at the hospital after midnight. She stays while Jenna goes home to sleep. When Jenna returns in the morning, she leaves a note on the fridge for Julie, who hasn't been home all night.

By six a.m., Bill is acting like himself, or at least the version of himself they have all grown used to since the last surgery. He needs the transfusions more and more frequently. Jenna thinks she remembers the doctors saying this would happen toward the end. There's only so much to be done now, his body too frail for another surgery to repair the leaking. The transfusions are all they can do to keep him lucid and alive until he simply isn't anymore.

For days following each surgery, Bill had to be restrained in his hospital bed, wide Velcro bands across his wrists and ankles. They needed to be secured tightly, and generally they were, but once he'd managed to get loose. He took a serious fall that time, breaking his nose. When asked where he'd been going, he explained he was getting ice cream. Jenna started bringing ice cream into the hospital after that.

Jenna's mother goes home to rest while Jenna stays with Bill. She'll be back for his release in the afternoon. All morning, they watch the early news programs run, one into another. Jenna wishes he could still play cards with the lazy patience he'd had on rainy days in her childhood. Go Fish is the only game he could follow now, and Jenna doesn't have the patience for that.

At lunch, they bring him a tray of food with different colored mush in each compartment. He puts a bite of each thing onto the fork, and Jenna makes a face.

"It all goes to the same place," he reminds her. Since she was little, she has always hated her food touching, and Bill used to tease her.

He slows after the first few bites.

"I can get you something else."

"Nah." He sets the fork down and sits back into his pillows. "Not so hungry."

Jenna picks up the tray and moves it to a table closer to the door. She sits in the chair beside him and looks up at the television in the corner. "Do you need your glasses back?" He had taken them off to eat.

Bill turns and lets her help him get them on. As she does it, she realizes this is something he can do by himself. She's overstepping and he's humoring her.

With their faces close together, Bill reaches out and strokes her hair. "Getting longer," he says. "Like your mother's when I met her. She was so beautiful."

Jenna smiles at the second-hand compliment.

"I knew right away I had to make her mine." He cocks an eyebrow at her.

Jenna laughs, unused to him talking like this. "Really? Was it love at first sight?"

"Oh, yes."

If pushed to consider it, Jenna doesn't believe in love at first sight. She thinks it is a coincidence when an immediate attraction happens to work out.

"But wait a minute." Her eyebrows knit together slowly. "Mom had short hair when you met." Jenna's mother has never had long hair in all the years since Jenna was born. "Maybe you're thinking of a picture you saw."

He becomes flustered. Why had she corrected him? What purpose did it serve to underline his confusion?

"Oh," he says. "I guess you're right." He shakes his head like a man emerging from a pool, shaking the water from his hair. She pictures Bill healthy, the way he looked in his swim trunks only a few summers ago—how his skin tanned so quickly, the lean muscles of his chest. Now, the same body is pale and soft, covered in long ragged marks, scars left by well-meaning surgeons who had carved into his flesh, making things worse. "Things are jumbled up," he says.

"It's okay. It all ends up in the same place." She isn't exactly sure what she means, but it sounds right. And it seems to help. Bill's expression unclouds.

He looks past her. "Sam!"

Jenna turns, certain this is another instance of Bill's altered thinking. But no. Sam stands in the doorway wearing navy blue dress pants and a yellow tie.

"Mr. Shaw," he says, walking in. "How are you feeling?"

"I'm doing great," Bill insists. "Yourself?"

"Can't complain." Sam turns to Jenna and nods hello. He turns back to Bill, setting a Dunkin' Donuts bag on the table by the bed. "I wasn't sure what you liked. I got a few different choices. Are they letting you eat?"

Bill looks to Jenna for the answer "Let's check with the doctor first," she says. "There's so much sugar in those things."

"She knows donuts," Bill says, and it sounds like an insult. A dig at her weight. But Jenna knows this isn't what he means; it wouldn't occur to him.

She peeks into the bag. "Looks like he got you a Boston Kreme like you like." She moves the bag to another table. "For later," she whispers, winking at Bill as he frowns.

"I get to go home in a few hours," Bill tells Sam proudly.

"Good for you. I'm glad to hear it."

Bill's head bobs up and down, making him look like one of those dashboard figurines.

"Well, look, I should get back to work. Wanted to pop my head in and say hey."

"I'll walk you to the elevator," Jenna says quickly, and she sees Bill smirk out of the corner of her eye.

They don't speak to each other in the hallway. At the door to the elevator, Sam turns to her without pressing the button.

"How did you know we were here?" she asks.

"I went to your house first. Your mom said you'd be here."

"Why did you come?" It sounds rude, but she's truly baffled.

"After last night, I was worried about him...And you."

"Me?"

"I know. You're fine." He smiles easily, like this is any other Tuesday, like they're sitting on a park bench. "I wanted to see for myself."

"Sam." She wants to get this over with quickly. "I don't think I can do this right now. My life is too crazy."

"Do what?"

"This." Jenna waves her hand back and forth between the two of them.

"I'm bringing your dad some donuts." He says this with a straight face, but his eyes dance.

Jenna bites her lip to keep from smiling. She presses the button for the elevator and walks away.

***

"Tell me about this boy."

"What boy?"

Barbara freezes halfway across the kitchen floor, giving her daughter a look of absolute incredulousness.

"He's no one." It isn't only that she doesn't want to talk about him—she hasn't come up with her own answer to this question—she has other things on her mind. She's getting tired of her sister's abdication of responsibility. Julie spends more and more nights out of the house and when she does stay home, she sleeps until noon. "I don't understand how she's paying her bills."

"Who?"

Jenna rolls her eyes. Her mother knows exactly who she's talking about.

"I mean, I know she doesn't have to pay rent, but she has other expenses. A car. A credit card."

Barbara scrapes butter onto her toast. "I gave her some money a little while ago," she says, guiltily, not looking up.

Jenna throws up her hands.

"She hadn't paid her car payment in a couple of months." She says this defensively.

"What? Doesn't she know they can repossess her car?"

Barbara shrugs.

"You can't keep rescuing her every time she gets in a mess."

"She said she was going to ask your father. The *biological*."

Jenna shakes her head. "She'd never really do that. She must have been bluffing."

"Well, she seemed pretty serious."

"Well, let her. When's the last time he paid for anything besides bus fare?" Jenna has never asked him for anything. Not ever. But then, Jenna wouldn't ask her mother to pay her car payment either so who knows what Julie would do?

"I don't want him to think I can't take care of you girls."

"It's not your job to take care of her, Mom. She's twenty-one years old. When is she going to start taking care of herself?"

"I don't know, Jenna. But can't we worry about this later? How I've failed as a mother and blah blah blah?"

"That isn't what I'm saying."

"Let's focus on something more pleasant. Like this boy." Barbara hides her smile in her coffee cup.

Jenna sighs.

"He was all dressed up. What does he do?"

"Something at the bank. But it doesn't matter. We're not seeing each other anymore."

"Why not? What's wrong with him?"

"Nothing. He's a nice guy. I don't know." Jenna gets up and puts her bowl in the sink.

"He was cute."

"My head's not in it."

"It's not about your head, silly."

She remembers something. "You know what Bill told me yesterday?" She sits at the table again.

"No, what?" Barbara brushes a scattering of crumbs into her palm, then sprinkles them back onto her plate. She looks up at Jenna.

"He said it was love at first sight with you. He knew he had to have you."

"Aw." Barbara smiles, but her eyes are wet. "So sweet."

"Was it like that for you too?"

She nods. "An unstoppable force beyond my control."

It was hard for Jenna to think of her mother this way, as someone capable of an intense romantic drama. How could she? At five years old, Jenna had seen Bill as a nuisance, a distraction. Her mother told them it was nice to have another grown-up to talk to. And at first, it had seemed like a harmless thing to allow. But the more time Bill spent with her, with all of them, the more Jenna saw him as a threat to the delicate balance of their new lives.

After the divorce, they had all moved back to New Hampshire to be closer to her mother's parents. She can't remember missing her father or the house in Ohio, but she does remember the feeling of chaos that evaporated as they got settled, feeling more secure with each purchase of heavy furniture and the filling of closets. As far as Jenna was concerned, Bill could only disturb this newly achieved peace.

Julie and Jenna took turns faking stomachaches, so Billy had to call restaurants and interrupt their dates. They behaved horribly whenever Billy babysat them, until he resisted their mother's requests. They told her stories of how Billy mistreated them while she was away, and only some were true.

"Did you try to stop it?" Jenna asks.

"I did. At first."

"Because of us?"

Barbara pulls herself from the wistful daydream that has her staring off into middle distance. "Sure. I wanted to be sure it was right for everyone. I was always arguing with him about timing. But Bill wouldn't be put off. He fought for me."

Bill fought for all of them, Jenna thinks. She feels ashamed remembering all the hoops she made him jump through. He was willing to love them all, right from the beginning, and he was met with challenges every step of the way. Julie and Jenna acted like brats in Bill's presence, throwing tantrums and refusing to acknowledge the valiant attempts he made to be let into their world.

"So, he wore you down?"

Barbara sighs. "Not really. I tried living without him." She shrugs. "It wasn't as good."

Jenna's smile is fleeting as it dawns on her, that's exactly what's coming.

Chapter Five

The doctor's waiting room smells like Lysol, which to Jenna, smells like death.

When she and Julie were nine, they were allowed to get a pair of Siberian hamsters. They were adorable but so hyper they never let her hold them. They ran up and down her arms, jumping from one hand to the other. If Jenna tried to keep them still for even a moment, they pinched her with their little front teeth—never hard enough to draw blood, but enough to make her question her love for them. It wasn't long before she thought of them as no better than rats, smaller but just as filthy. Jenna and Julie argued over whose turn it was to clean the cage, changing the smelly, damp sawdust lining the bottom.

Jenna still remembers the excitement she felt the first time one of the hamsters let her hold him. He laid still on her hand, his eyelids at half-mast as she ran her fingertips over his soft coat. The excitement was short lived as she realized his hind end was smeared with green poop. After he died, his brother ran around him and over him without showing the slightest sign of grief. They scrubbed the cage with Lysol to keep the other hamster from getting sick. A week later, he was dead as well, and the smell of Lysol lingered.

In the corner of the waiting room, a grandfather is speaking Spanish to a little boy speaking baby talk. Jenna understands neither. They're giggling.

The door to her left clicks open. "Jenna Smiley?"

Jenna has always hated her last name. People always ask her to smile. Or worse, they note the name isn't fitting. She took Helen Reed's feminist theory class last semester, and they discussed the sexist implications of women changing their last names when they marry. Jenna sees it as one of the few perks.

She stands and follows the woman with the clipboard. Nurse? Physician's Assistant? She shows Jenna into a little room with an examining table covered in paper. Folded on top is a paper dress.

"I'm Elaine. Have a seat."

Jenna sits in the only available chair while Elaine sits on a rolling stool by a computer and starts asking questions about her periods and what medications she's on.

"Is there anything specific you want to talk to the doctor about today?"

"Nope." It's her annual visit, scheduled last year. Jenna figures she should keep doctor's appointments while she still has insurance. She's due to join the ranks of the uninsured after she graduates. If she graduates.

"Go ahead and change. The doctor will be in shortly."

Jenna nods. She looks at her watch, aware she starts her shift in less than an hour. She wishes she could spend all her time at home with Bill, watching television and listening to his stories. He's become much more talkative, more willing to share. A side effect of his meds or general confusion Jenna is taking advantage of. She wonders if she should feel more guilty.

She pulls her clothes off as fast as she can, dreading the idea of the doctor coming in while she has her shirt over her head. With or without clothes is fine, but there's something inexplicably mortifying about the halfway point. She sits on the examining table.

Time is passing infuriatingly quickly. It seems impossible she hasn't spoken to Julie in a week, a feat managed only by her busy schedule. Julie is rarely awake before Jenna leaves for work in the morning. They've been communicating through day-glow orange, passive aggressive Post-it notes left for each other on the kitchen table. Julie's were annoyingly cheerful, followed by several unnecessary exclamation points; Jenna keeps her messages short and to the point, her forced civility its own sort of hyperbole.

A small cabinet with a sink stands in the corner of the room. On the counter, next to a red plastic container for needle disposal and a box of tissues, there's a three-dimensional model of a pregnant woman. The plastic torso has a detachable plastic fetus, curled up and pink, clearly in the final trimester. There's hardly room for the rest of the torso's innards, and it's hard for Jenna to imagine two babies sharing that cramped space.

Jenna and Julie were born two months early. They spent the first three months of their lives in the hospital, in incubators under warming lamps, as if they were baby birds. Jenna weighed three pounds, five ounces. Julie weighed two pounds, three ounces. If anyone could feel guilt for something they'd done before they were born, it's Jenna.

Jenna believes Julie's helplessness made them close as children, then pushed them further and further apart as they grew up. Jenna can't remember a time when she didn't feel responsible for her sister. Julie has always been the underdog, the good-hearted idiot who can't be blamed for messing up. Whenever Julie fails at anything in life, Jenna feels as if it is her own failure too. She feels somehow culpable for her sister's mistakes.

Jenna stretches her legs out in front of her, noting the unflattering look of her white ankle socks with the paper gown. She pulls them off, pads over to the chair in the corner and tucks them under her folded clothing. The tile is quite cold on her bare feet, and before she has returned to sit on the examining table, she reconsiders. Who is she trying to impress? She retrieves her socks and puts them back on quickly.

The girls were separated after kindergarten because the teacher thought Julie's reliance on Jenna might not be in her best interest. But by then, it was already too late. There may have been a brief period when Julie tried to keep up, a time when Jenna remembers feeling ashamed of her good grades. And then

Julie seemed to surrender any sort of competition. She wasn't ready to move on to second grade when her sister was.

Again, Jenna checks the time on her wrist.

Unfortunately, unlike Julie, Jenna has to pay her bills. No one is going to swoop in and pay them for her. She still finds it impossible to believe Julie would ever ask their father for money.

The *biological* didn't contribute a nickel toward college, not even books. Instead, Jenna had to take on loans. An amount she can't bear to contemplate. She got them deferred so that, for now, she doesn't have to. As long as she returns to school in the spring, she'll be fine. Until she graduates. Eventually, there will be no way to delay the eternal monthly bills, and her sociology degree ensures a salary that will never cover them.

It feels wrong to think about the future, to plan for spring semester. They are all gritting their teeth to get beyond this tough time. Waiting to get to the other side. Which is? Life without Bill.

The paper rustles beneath her as she shifts on the table, holding her hands in her lap, trying to look natural.

There are two quick knocks on the door before it opens. The doctor steps inside. "Hi, Jenna! Got a smile for me?"

***

The walls of Jenna's bedroom are bright orange. It's her favorite color. In contrast, the furniture is dark, and her bedspread is a pale, multi-colored paisley. She has an array of hand-painted glass ornaments hanging by the window. She never bothered to take them down when she moved out. They reminded her of high school, of who she was then.

The girls had redecorated their rooms when Bill was on one of his home-improvement kicks. He pulled up all the carpet one day while they were at school. He hadn't thought to run it by them first, didn't understand someone could form a sentimental attachment to flooring. He'd installed Pergo. It looked like hardwood but sounded different.

Jenna stretches out on her bed with a magazine. She's changed into her favorite pair of overalls. They're a gorgeous mess of orange and purple paint on faded blue denim.

The paint was Barbara's idea, a way to appease the girls. She laughed at Bill's obliviousness: Girls were sentimental about everything. They made a family trip to Home Depot to collect paint chips. Julie's walls are lavender.

Bill painted all the edges, unscrewed the light switch covers. He taped the baseboards and stood on a ladder, careful not to get paint on the ceiling. He left Jenna the wide expanses in between.

He showed her how to paint vulgar words on the walls, then cover them so no one would ever know. His words weren't terribly bad—like "ass" and "bull crap." Julie had come to the door when Jenna had painted "boob" across the wall. Bill was chuckling. Julie shook her head. "You guys are *weird.*"

If she looks close, Jenna thinks she can almost make it out.

"Does that magazine have a perfume sample in it?" Julie wanders into Jenna's room and sits at the foot of the bed.

"Several." Jenna flips the page, not looking up.

"Are you going to stay mad at me forever?"

Jenna sighs. "What are we? Twelve?"

"I said I was sorry."

Yeah, Jenna thinks. *And what has changed?* But there's no use in saying it. Being mad at Julie is like spitting in the wind. She looks up. "'It's always me who ends up getting wet.'"

"Huh?"

"It's a lyric. Popped into my head. What's it from?"

"Oh." Julie sucks on the ends of her hair. Their mother used to threaten to cut it short so it wouldn't reach her mouth. She never followed through. "Sting. 'Every Little Thing She Does Is Magic.'"

Jenna nods. "You made me think of it."

"Aw." Julie drops the strand of hair. "Friends again?"

"Okay."

Julie smiles, an almost indiscernible tension abandoning her shoulders. "We should do something tonight. I'm bored."

As a little girl, Julie needed Jenna's help with most things, until she overcame her shyness and learned to cash in on being pretty. Julie barely got through high school, graduating a year behind Jenna, but she always had a boyfriend.

"Where's Brad?" Jenna asks, surprised she remembers his name.

Julie groans and melts across the mattress. "I'm letting him stew."

Jenna looks out the window at the darkness. "It's late."

"It's not even ten o'clock," Julie whines.

Jenna shrugs and flips the page of her magazine again.

"You're no fun."

"Yep. That's me."

Her *Cosmo* promises *Wild New Sex Tricks!* Jenna scans the page with little interest. *Clitoral Stimulation! Reverse Cowgirl! Clench the PC Muscles!* There's never really anything new.

"I wish you were my boyfriend so I could make you go out and get me a milkshake," Julie says.

"That's something boyfriends do?"

"Totally."

Jenna's cell phone rings. She glances at the number and puts it on her nightstand, unanswered.

Julie lifts her head. "Who are we avoiding?"

"No one. Unknown number."

Julie lets her head fall back. "Probably a telemarketer."

"Probably." Jenna can't tell the truth. Julie would never let it drop.

***

Later, checking her messages, Jenna presses her ear to the receiver, closer to Sam's voice. "Hey, Jenna. It's me." Me? Already? Jenna thinks this is presumptuous. "I know you have a lot on your plate right now, and I don't want to make things worse. I mean, making you nauseous all the time and all." Here, he clears his throat. "I *am* sorry about that. But I thought we had fun. Didn't we? And maybe I could stop. Making you sick." He chuckles, but it turns into a groan. "Look, I'll leave you alone if that's what you want… Is it? What you want?" He pauses here, as if waiting for an answer. "Well, you have my number."

Jenna feels as if she has swallowed a menthol cough drop in its entirety.

Boys were Julie's one area of expertise and Jenna let her have them. After a few awkward attempts, Jenna lost her virginity when she was in high school to a boy who was only a friend. They pretended to be more than that long enough to get the sex out of the way. And that's how it felt—not like she had given away something sacred leaving her damaged, dirty, and used. Also, not like she had become a different person or had entered womanhood.

Jenna felt unburdened. It was like a question answered, leaving her free to concentrate on other things.

And she had. She didn't date at all in college. If asked, she would say she was too busy with academics and social activities. The truth was, she never thought about it. A girl at a party kissed her once and, drunk on Kool-Aid and vodka, Jenna let her. It reminded Jenna of third-grade slumber parties when the girls made out with their hands. Their teeth clicked together, and Jenna thought vaguely, *not this either*.

But now, suddenly and out of nowhere, Jenna's feeling all the sickening clichés she took some degree of pride in being immune to. She doesn't understand whether it's caused by something unique about Sam or is simply some essential change in who she is—and she's not convinced the change is an improvement. When she looks around, she doesn't see many enviable love stories.

Whatever the source, Jenna can't think of a worse time to be wrestling with such nonsense. Her plate *is* full.

When she closes her eyes, she sees his. The way he looks at her like he knows her, like he's calling bullshit; how he knows when to push for answers and when to let her be.

She sits on the edge of her bed, holding the phone in her lap. Sam's number is on the screen, all she has to do is press *Send*. And yet, it might be easier to delete his number, put the phone in her bag, and go to sleep.

It's the easier thing, but it's not what she wants to do. It's completely up to her, and she feels lightheaded with the power of that, the knowledge that her fate is in her hands for once.

***

Jenna and Sam sit on the grass along the edge of Massabesic Lake. For several minutes, the only noise is the slurping of their ice cream cones.

"We were never allowed to get jimmies when I was little," Jenna says.

"Why?"

"Too messy."

"Wow. You have sad, sad stories."

The weather is nice for October. Jenna wears jeans and a short-sleeved shirt. The breeze is cool, but the sun is warm. "Is the phrase 'Indian Summer' racist?"

Sam thinks for a moment. "Not sure what the literal meaning is. But probably."

"Maybe something about the weather being deceptive?"

"Those crafty little Indians."

"Not crafty enough."

"No, I guess not. I bet they wish they'd had a tougher immigration policy."

Jenna laughs. Immigration is a hot topic of debate these days, as the country gears up for another election. The world chugs along like it always does, and it strikes Jenna as unfair. Cruel, even.

"How's your dad?" It's like he knows what she's thinking sometimes. It's unsettling.

"He's been good. And my mother's been home all week which makes him happy."

"Good."

Something has changed between them. The butterflies aren't gone, but this is different. By agreeing to go out with him again, Jenna feels some broader agreement has been negotiated. To give him a chance despite the part of her that is terrified. To resist the feeling she gets when she looks in his eyes, when he smiles, when he touches her. There is something safe there, easy and comforting. And yet she must fight the urge to run. Maybe that's what she has agreed to do.

"How's Dunkin's?"

She groans. Yesterday, Molly asked Jenna about her OBGYN and acted concerned when Jenna didn't have an answer. Apparently, Molly's mother works as a receptionist for one of the city's best.

"That good, huh?" Sam leans forward as his cone drips into the grass. He shoves the rest of it into his mouth.

"My coworkers think I'm pregnant."

Sam coughs. "What?"

Jenna laughs. "I'm not," she states firmly. "You know my stupid uniform?"

He nods and she tells him the story as he gathers their paper trash.

"It spun out of control," Jenna concludes. "Now my coworkers are knitting me booties."

Sam stretches out, his hands clasped behind his head. "I never would have guessed you were such a good liar."

Jenna smiles. "See, you don't know me."

"Oh, but I do." Sam winks at her. "The day I came in, your coworkers thought I was hitting on a pregnant woman?"

"Is that what you were doing? Hitting on me?"

"Um." Sam shields his eyes with one hand as he looks up at her. "Yeah!" he says as if he is saying *Duh!* "And it worked too. I am so smooth."

"You think so?"

"I got your digits, didn't I?"

Jenna lies beside him in the grass, the sides of their arms touching. "Molly asked if you were the father."

"What did you tell her?"

"I said you were a friend."

"Somehow that hurts my feelings."

"Well, that's what you were. Then."

Sam turns his whole body to face her. "And what am I now?"

"I don't know yet."

He reaches out and brushes her hair off her forehead. "Well, I'm glad you called me." He leans in and kisses her, his fingers entangled in the hair behind her neck. He pulls back. "Tell Molly I'm the father. I'm tired of you being ashamed of me."

Jenna laughs.

***

When he takes her home that night, the house is lit up. Light spills from the kitchen window onto the front lawn, a figure standing within the frame. As they approach the front door, Jenna sees it's her mother doing the dishes.

"Am I allowed to kiss you with your mother watching?" Sam asks.

"Um, yeah, maybe not." Jenna has never kissed a boy in front of her family. The idea makes her itch.

Sam sticks his hands in his pockets and scuffs his sneakers on the porch. "Damn. I really want to kiss you again."

Jenna shakes her head and smiles. They spent the entire day kissing. In the grass. In the car. And yet, she feels the same.

Barbara pulls the door open and Jenna steps back, surprised. "I'm not here," she says.

"That would be nice," Jenna agrees, giving her mother a forced smile.

"Nice to see you again, Mrs. Shaw," Sam says politely.

"Please. Call me Barbara," she says all flirty. She catches another look from Jenna. "Oh. Bill wanted me to invite Sam to the party tomorrow. He made me promise. So, that's all. I'm gone." She pulls the door closed, leaving them alone on the porch again.

"Party?"

"It's Bill's birthday. My stepbrother's coming with his family. It'll be a crazy day. You don't have to come."

"Sounds like a blast. Unless you'd rather I didn't. I mean, if it's family."

"No, I mean, if Bill invited you." She shrugs. In the back of her mind, it occurs to her this might be a ploy of her mother's, a way to check out the boy she's dating.

"Okay. What should I bring?" Sam asks.

"Nothing. Really. There is going to be too much food already." A wave of anxiety hits her. "I feel like I must warn you. My family? Nuts."

"That's exactly what I'd expect from meeting you."

Before Jenna can formulate a response, Sam pulls her toward him and kisses her. He releases her quickly. "She wasn't looking," he whispers, pointing to the window.

***

Sunday is another warm day, full of sunshine and the smells of autumn. The oak tree out back has reddish-brown leaves, some of which are scattered in the grass. Jenna and Bill Jr. move Bill's blue chair into the backyard. Her mother and Annie lay the food out on the table. Cold cuts, chips, and hummus and veggies from Annie's garden. Julie plays with Lucas, giving him piggyback rides and tickling him while he squeals.

Any suspicion she had that inviting Sam was her mother's idea quickly disappears. Bill keeps asking if Sam is coming, and when, and if she's sure. He doesn't stop asking until Sam shows up, at one p.m. on the dot, with a card and balloons.

She shakes her head at him.

"I couldn't come empty-handed," he says defensively.

She pulls him inside and he catches her at the waist, stepping close for a kiss hello.

"Bill thinks you're his new buddy," she says. "He's been talking about you all morning."

"Really?" Sam struts slightly as she leads him out the back.

"Look who's here!" Jenna announces, throwing the door open.

Sam and Bill shake hands and exchange greetings.

Jenna ties the balloons to the patio chair beside Bill and Lucas begs to have one for himself.

"Those are Grampa's," Annie tells him.

"Oh, he can have one," Bill pleads his case, winking at him.

Jenna bends down and ties one of the strings to Lucas' wrist and they all watch as he bounces happily away.

"Well, that was a hit." Jenna squeezes Sam's hand.

"Balloons," Barbara says, "I didn't think of them. Thank you, Sam."

"Jenna told me you'd be covered for food," Sam says, and they sit around the table.

"I'd say so," Bill agrees, nodding at the spread.

***

Jenna carries the cake down the steps carefully. They got candles with numbers so there are fewer wicks. The lit Six and Eight flicker as she tiptoes toward the table, Norman dancing at her feet.

"Norman. Come." Bill's voice is a deep growl, and Norman obeys at once.

Julie places a cone shaped hat on Bill's head, pulling the elastic under his chin. He looks at her with skepticism. She replies by bending down and blowing her party horn at him. It unrolls, tapping the end of his nose and making a slight wheeze.

Jenna places the cake at the center of the table, and they sing. Everyone helps him blow out the candles, his attempt just for show. Jenna wonders about his wish, if he remembered to wish for anything and what it might be. But she doesn't ask. She can't help but think of these things as the *last*. The last cake, the last candles, the last party. She pushes the thought away, reminding herself she thought these same things last year and was wrong.

But she's especially grateful for the good weather. And the chocolate cake is moist and delicious. And there are no fights, no broken dishes. Lucas' balloon is still tied to his wrist, drooping slightly. And she remembers the camera. As the sun dips below the tree branches, Jenna breathes a sigh of relief for the perfect day. If this must be the last, it will be a good one to remember.

***

As the night grows cooler, Bill Jr. and Sam bring the recliner into the house. Jenna and her mother help Bill up the three steps from the yard and follow them into the den.

"You must be tired, dear," Barbara says as she eases him back into his chair. "Quite a day."

"Best birthday ever," Bill says, and the room is filled with soft, melancholy laughter.

Bill Jr. lifts Lucas so he can kiss his grandfather goodnight. As they say their goodbyes, there are offers to help clean up. Jenna's mother assures them she has all under control. Julie walks the three of them out to their car.

Sam shakes Bill's hand. "Thank you for inviting me."

Bill nods. "Take care of my girl," he says.

"Bill," Jenna flushes. This has caught her off guard, coming out of the blue like many of Bill's thoughts these days. "I can take care of myself," She tries to say this without sounding defensive, but she isn't sure she manages.

Bill sucks his teeth to convey how ridiculous she sounds.

Jenna bends to kiss Bill's cheek. "Goodnight, you." He smiles at her, and she rolls her eyes. She follows Sam to the driveway, struck silent.

"Wait 'til you meet my mother." He says this to make her feel better, she knows, but in it, she hears expectation.

Without thinking, she walks to the passenger's side of his car.

"You coming with me?" He walks around to the driver's side, talking to her over the roof.

"Oh." She lets go of the door handle. "Can I?"

"Always."

She slides beside him. "I want to see where you live."

He raises his eyebrows. "Okay."

"That's not code for sex," she clarifies.

"Then forget it," he says, backing out of the drive. "Anyone who stands on my front doorstep must have sex with me. It's the rule."

"Ah."

"Look, it's hard on everyone. Take the UPS guy, for example. But a rule's a rule."

"You're hilarious," she deadpans.

Sam huffs dramatically. "Fine. I guess I can make an exception this once."

Jenna waits a moment. "You done?"

"Yeah."

***

"I wasn't expecting company," he says, fitting the key into the lock. "So, it might be a little messy."

It isn't. Sam lives on the first floor of a two-story house. In his kitchen, there's a single glass in the sink. All the others are drying on a rack, the counters are bare and wiped clean.

Sam lets her inside while he pulls the mail from the box. She wanders from the kitchen to the small living room where he has a futon and a television set and a coffee table. She pokes her head into the bathroom while he stands at the kitchen table and shuffles through his mail.

"What are you learning about me?"

"You're a neat freak."

"Yep," he admits, ripping open a red envelope from Netflix. Jenna walks toward him. "Whatcha got there?"

"The Station Agent. The Netflix rating system suggested it." He tells her how they have different ratings for movies they think he will like based on how he has rated previous movies and they're always considerably lower than the general rating. "It makes me feel bad, like Netflix is accusing me of being too picky. This isn't how I want to be seen."

"It's a computer," Jenna reminds him.

"I know. I don't like to feel judged." He goes to the sink and turns on the faucet.

She walks into his bedroom. A framed print of Picasso's *The Rest* hangs on the wall above the headboard. "You make your bed!" She sits down on it, running her hand over the top of the dark green comforter. He stands in the doorway, the light from the kitchen and the darkness of the bedroom obscures his features, making him an anonymous tall shadow.

She lies back and pats the space beside her. Sam steps closer, slowly. "But you said." He stands over her, eyeing her warily.

"I know what I said, and I meant it. But it's just a bed." She pats the bed again.

"Just a bed." He lies down beside her.

She kisses him, aware this is the first time she hasn't waited for him to kiss her. Their hands are in each other's hair, their breathing coming louder and faster. They roll and shift, and he's on top of her. She pulls his shirt over his head and slides her hands across his bare chest, a scattering of wiry tufts beneath her fingertips.

"You have the perfect amount of chest hair."

"I think so," he agrees, looking down at himself. "I did a survey."

He slides his hands under her shirt, and she loses herself in the rhythm of his tongue moving against hers.

She pulls back and looks into his eyes. "Pants stay on."

He nods quickly, unbuttoning her shirt, letting his mouth travel down her neck, exploring the soft skin of her shoulders as he removes her bra. His mouth finds her nipple, first one and then the other. His hands are moving along her thighs, alternately rubbing them softly then gripping them tightly, pressing his fingers into them.

Jenna's hand moves toward the waist of her jeans. Her fingers graze the button.

"Pants stay on," he whispers, circling her wrist in his fingers, gently pulling her hand away and covering her mouth with his.

Chapter Six

On the days when her shift is over late enough, Jenna drives to Sam's house before her own. Sometimes she has to get home to Bill, so she stays long enough to kiss him and laugh for a few minutes. Sometimes he cooks dinner, nothing fancy, and sometimes she brings over food from a drive-through. She knows what he likes at all the chains: Chalupas and Dr. Pepper at Taco Bell, a Whopper and vanilla shake at Burger King. On the nights when her mother's home, she might stay to watch the latest selection from Netflix, curled up beside him on the futon.

She never stays over, though. He hasn't asked her, and she isn't sure she wants him to.

When he hears her car pulling into the driveway, he looks out his front door, opening it as she walks up the front stairs.

"How was work?" He turns the kitchen chair backward and straddles it.

"Same old." Jenna lifts a DVD in its return envelope. "What was this?"

"*Maria Full of Grace.*"

"Any good?" She sits down beside him, shrugging off her jacket.

"Eh." He shrugs. "I found its lack of nudity and explosions challenging attention-wise, but it was good. Subtitles."

Jenna nods, mock-serious.

"Is your mother home?" he asks. This is their shorthand for: *Can you stay?*

"She is. Want to go out?"

"Sort of." He smiles. "I'm having dinner at my mother's. Come?"

She feels tricked. It's too late to use Bill as an excuse.

"Come."

They take her car since it is parked behind his, and it's still warm. They're in the last days of October, and all the sunny afternoons and warm evenings are gone until spring. Sam calls his mother on the way to let her know Jenna's coming. He bats at the dice hanging from the rearview mirror and waves off her protests his mother might want more warning.

Sam's mother is a tiny woman. She wears yoga pants and a halter top, her hair dyed the color of merlot, cut close to her scalp and standing up like spikes on a cactus. She kisses the air around Sam's face.

"I've been doing my video," she explains, punching an invisible assailant and throwing an unexpected high kick that apparently takes him down.

"Whoa, Mom. Let me see the guns."

She flexes her right bicep and growls.

"Nice." He nods, looking at Jenna for affirmation.

"Oh. Wow." Jenna becomes aware her eyes are open too wide, her eyebrows high on her forehead. She blinks and tries to adjust.

"Jenna, do you like cats?" Sam's mother asks.

"Uh." This is not the quiz she was expecting. "I do, yes."

Sam takes Jenna's coat as his mother leads them down the hall.

"By the way, I'm Cindy," she says. With one hand on the doorknob, she turns to them and holds a finger to her lips. "They're sleeping."

Inside, in a cardboard box lined with newspaper, there's a fat orange cat and five kittens. The mother cat opens her eyes when the three of them enter the room, but she doesn't raise her head.

"When did you get these?" Sam asks.

"Just last night. They had nowhere else to go."

"They never do." Sam looks over at Jenna. "She fosters for the Humane Society. They're always suckering her."

"Look at them," Cindy coos. "Who could say no?"

Jenna thinks she could. She remembers the sweet puppy smell Norman had when they first brought him home. She used to lean into his yawns. But the cats smell like urine and well, cat.

On a coffee table, there's an arrangement of tarot cards. "You do readings?" Jenna asks.

"Oh, sometimes. Are you familiar with tarot?"

"I had friends in college who played around with it." Jenna points at one of the cards. "That one doesn't look good."

"The Ten of Swords." Cindy shakes her head solemnly. The card depicts a body lying face down with ten swords sticking out along his spine. "It generally refers to a punishment for one's misdeeds, a final loss. Every card has both good and bad in it, and this can signify the end of pain from a specific source. It's now time to learn from your mistakes. But I never like to see this card."

"Whose reading was this?" Sam asks.

"Miranda. I'm afraid she has a tough road ahead."

"Who's Miranda?" Jenna whispers.

"From her soaps." Sam smiles at her, daring her to laugh.

"I could do a relationship reading for the two of you," Cindy offers enthusiastically.

Luckily, Sam squashes this idea. It isn't as if Jenna believes in tarot, but she imagines it would be stressful to have their budding relationship analyzed by Sam's mother.

Cindy shrugs. "Suit yourself. Why don't you set the table while I change? I made chili."

Jenna follows Sam to the kitchen. "Do you believe in that stuff?" she asks him.

Sam washes his hands at the sink. "I don't *not* believe in it." He shrugs. "Growing up, my mother went through these religious spurts. We were Catholic for a while, then Protestant, then Episcopalian. Long periods between where we weren't anything at all. Maybe I believe in a little bit of everything."

Jenna has vague memories of attending church in Ohio before the divorce. On one of those Sundays, God called the *biological* to become a minister and leave his family. Since then, Jenna hasn't believed in much of anything.

Jenna washes her hands as Sam gets three bowls out of a cabinet.

"You lied," he says.

"What?" Jenna turns off the faucet and tries to read his expression.

"You don't really like cats."

Jenna laughs. "I don't *not* like them."

***

Cindy comes into the kitchen barefoot, wearing a pair of flared jeans with rainbows embroidered on the back pockets, the kind you buy in the junior's department. She places the pot of chili in the middle of the table. "Sam, can you grab the Tabasco sauce?" She sits down and makes motions for Jenna to take the seat across from her. "I start with mild, and you can season as spicy as you want. I used to love spicy foods, but now I get the heartburn." She makes a fist and thumps her chest.

Sam sits at the end of the table, between the two of them. He sets the bottle of Tabasco sauce by his bowl and serves the chili, starting with Jenna.

Cindy slices the corn bread. "Sam told me your dad's been sick. I'm real sorry about that."

Jenna nods, holding her bowl out. "That's enough," she tells Sam.

"I was about your age when I lost my mother." Cindy holds her bowl up as Sam spoons chili into it.

"I'm sorry."

"Thanks." Cindy pauses, thoughtful. "That's really all you can say about it. People always try to say more. To cheer you up. They mean well, but they end up saying the dumbest things."

Jenna blows on her spoon. "I overheard a friend of my sister's saying at least my dad had lived a full life."

"Right. As if that makes any of it better." Sam serves himself and adds Tabasco sauce before tasting.

"Most people can't handle each other's grief," Cindy says. "They want to talk you out of it."

Sam talks with his mouth full. "At least it wasn't a stick through your roof."

Jenna turns to him and makes a face.

"It's a family saying," he explains.

"My grandmother," Cindy says. "Once, she came over and caught my mother crying. My mother was dying of cancer, and my grandmother told her to stop feeling sorry for herself. Can you imagine?" She looks from Jenna to Sam, still incredulous after all these years. "Then she told her during the storm the night before, a stick came through the roof and *that* was the kind of thing worth crying about. Said she should count her blessings she hadn't had a stick come through her roof."

"Wow." Jenna shakes her head.

"Of course, she didn't mean it. Her daughter was dying, she must have been terrified. People don't want to face reality, and they say stupid shit."

Sam sprinkles more Tabasco in his bowl. "Like, God won't give you more than you can bear."

"The person who says that has never been through anything unbearable," Jenna says.

Cindy nods. "Or I know exactly how you feel. Love that one."

"Everything happens for a reason."

"It's all for the best."

"They're in a better place now."

"She was too good for this world."

"Or, at least you have time to say goodbye," Jenna says, and her voice cracks.

Cindy reaches across the table, covering Jenna's hand. "People should keep their damn mouths shut."

***

Back at Sam's apartment, they sit on opposite ends of the futon, and he pulls her

feet into his lap. His hands slide up the inside of her pant leg and knead her calf.

"So, what did you think of my mom?" he asks.

"She was so nice."

"So, see? Your family doesn't corner the market on crazy."

Jenna feigns confusion. "I *liked* her."

"Uh-huh. I love her. She's my favorite person. She's also a little cuckoo."

He runs his knuckle from the heel of her foot to the pad of her big toe. She giggles. "Well, I will say I understand now why you didn't flinch at the craziness in my family."

Sam sits back, satisfied.

"But really, she's great. Colorful. What's your dad like?" She pushes her other foot against his thigh, and he takes it between his warm palms.

"My real dad is fairly dull. I haven't seen much of him since I was a kid. I still see my stepdad though. We go to a Sox game every now and then, and when Tara comes home, we'll all have dinner as a family."

"That sounds nice. So, he and your mom still get along."

"Yeah, they're friends. My mom picked better the second time around."

"Mine too." He slides his hands up her other pant leg, a little higher than her knee this time. She smiles and shifts farther away. "Were you in the wedding? A ringbearer?"

"Nope. They went to Vegas."

"*Vegas?*"

"It wasn't a surprise. They told me what they were doing. But my mom said she felt private, just between them. What about you?"

"Julie and I were flower girls. It was about the only time I agreed to the matching outfit bullshit. The ceremony was short. They stood in the back yard under the oak tree. My brother gave her away."

"How old was he?"

"Fourteen?" Jenna closes her eyes. "It was the five of us. And the minister." She tries to remember why her grandmother wasn't there. "Very simple. No Elvis impersonators."

"Do you have pictures?"

"Yep."

"I bet you made an adorable flower girl." He moves closer to her, his hands sliding back up her thigh. This time, she doesn't move away.

***

The next night, Jenna goes straight home after work. Her mother's away on an overnight trip for work and Julie seems to have patched things up with her boyfriend, for now. It's Jenna's job to get Bill ready for bed.

"What did Julie make you for dinner?" Jenna finds a clean pair of pajamas in the drawer. She puts them on the bed beside him.

"Mac 'n cheese." He bends his elbows, raising his arms in surrender as she pulls off his T-shirt.

"That's it?" She helps him get his arms in the pajama top, buttoning it quickly, averting her eyes from the scars.

"I like mac 'n cheese." He stands up to pull down his pants. "It's the cheesiest."

"Uh-huh." Bill sits on the bed again as she disentangles his pants from around his ankles, tossing them into the laundry pile in the corner. "Did you get enough to eat?" She kneels, helping him get his feet through the leg holes.

"Yep." He stands, pulling the pajama bottoms up the rest of the way by himself. He sits down on the bed, his breathing labored.

Jenna narrows her eyes at him. "You sure?"

Bill nods, and Jenna leans past him to arrange his pillows. She holds his upper arms as he scoots back and leans against them. "You're mine," he says, smiling at her.

She straightens and smiles right back. "I sure am."

She hears the front door slam and Julie's angry footfalls up the stairs. *Trouble in paradise.*

"When you and Julie were born, you were so tiny. I could hold each one of you in my palm." Bill looks down at his hand, stretching out his fingers and cupping them for an imaginary newborn.

"But I don't think you knew us then," Jenna reminds him gently. She helps him slide his legs under the top sheet. She pushes the blanket to the side so it's within his reach when he gets cold later.

Bill scowls, shaking his head fiercely. Again, Jenna scolds herself for correcting him. It only seems to upset him.

"That's not true," Bill says angrily.

Jenna nods. "Okay. I'm sorry. Go ahead."

The tension leaves his face. "Your mother let me visit the hospital for a few hours." He lowers his voice to a raspy whisper. "I begged her to let me take you all away. Billy too. I didn't care he wasn't mine."

Jenna sits down on the edge of the bed, her eyebrows knit in concentration, trying to make his words make sense.

"But she wanted to honor her vows. She made me leave. I didn't want to!" He reaches for Jenna, crying. "I never would have left you if I'd had my way."

Jenna nods slowly. Her head is swimming.

"I promised your mother I'd never tell you." His eyes widened suddenly. "Don't tell her I told!" He sits forward, agitated.

"Of course," Jenna reassures, patting his arm. "Lie back, now."

He does as he's told. "I'm tired."

"I know. Long day."

Bill closes his eyes. "You're mine," he murmurs and drifts off.

Jenna spends a few useless moments smoothing out the top sheet as she tries to get control of her breathing. She stands slowly and stumbles out of the room, thinking: *Impossible.* It was such an elaborate story to create. Was it part of the dying process to recreate history the way you wished things had been?

She pulls his door closed, careful not to make a sound. She heads down the hall for the kitchen. Could it be true? Her body sways, and she presses a hand against the table to steady herself. She shakes her head. Out the window, she sees Julie's car in the driveway. She swipes the day's mail off the table and walks numbly out the door, down the front stairs.

In the car, she replays snippets of conversations from her life over and over in her mind. She files them into two categories and finds the stronger case: These are the crazy ramblings of a confused old man. It isn't true, can't be. At a red light, she organizes the mail in her lap from largest to smallest. At the next light, she decides that it makes no sense. This time she organizes by type: Coupons, credit card solicitors, charities, bills. Personal letters would go on top of the pile, but there are none of these.

Her breathing slows. It isn't true.

Sam opens the door before she can knock.

Jenna carries the mail into his apartment and Sam shuffles back into the kitchen where the refrigerator door hangs open. He takes a last look, then shuts it empty-handed.

"Hey."

"Hey," Jenna says. She feels like one of those exotic birds, the kind that learns to repeat common phrases without understanding their meaning.

"How was your day?" He opens the fridge again and leans into it, shuffling things around to see what's in the back.

Jenna tosses her keys onto the kitchen table and flips through the mail, this time sorting it by owner. "My day," she says, trailing off. She finds her name on an envelope from UNICEF, the kind with the return address labels. She always feels guilty using those labels without sending a donation. She holds the envelope over the trash can, then reconsiders.

Sam pulls out a jar of green olives. "How long have I had these?" he asks, idly.

As little as a nickel could save a child's life! the envelope says. Jenna uses her thumbnail to slice it open along the top edge.

Sam holds the jar up and squints at the label. "These the kind with pits in them?"

Jenna pulls the papers out and gasps. There's a nickel affixed to the first page.

"You okay?" Sam puts the jar down on the counter.

"I almost threw this away," Jenna murmurs.

Sam walks closer to look over her shoulder. "A nickel?"

"Yeah. They say it's enough money to save a child's life. And I almost threw it away!" Jenna turns to him, stricken.

Sam smiles at her. He's amused she is taking the matter so seriously.

"Think of all the nickels that get thrown away," she says, pulling the coin from the piece of paper, rubbing it between her thumb and first finger.

"It's a clever advertising strategy, baby. That's all." Sam stands behind her, putting his big hands on her shoulders. "They guilt enough people into sending money that it justifies the loss."

Jenna pulls out a chair and sits at the table. "That's awful." She imagines all those envelopes going into trash cans around

America. A gaunt, third-world baby dying with every careless flick of the wrist. "Awful," she says again, bringing her hands to her face and crying.

Sam stands for a moment in stunned silence. "Whoa, whoa, whoa," he says, turning her chair and kneeling on the floor in front of her. "Did I miss something?"

"It's Bill."

"What happened?"

"He's my father!"

"Okay. Yeah, I know."

"My real father."

"Oh, okay. That Bill."

"No. Bill. Lives in town, raised me my whole life, dying Bill. He's my father."

"Of course."

"No. Biologically."

Sam blinks. "I don't understand."

"Me neither." Jenna lays her head on the table. "It can't be true," she says, her voice smothered in the cradle of her arms. There are a million reasons to doubt him. And yet Jenna feels like the words Bill spoke were so obvious, like something she's known all along.

Sam strokes her hair and waits.

***

She sits on the futon, hugging her knees. She explains it to him slowly.

"That's what he said, but he doesn't know what he's saying. It's what the doctors said. He's hypoxic. He's not getting enough oxygen to his brain and his imagination is running wild."

She looks to him for confirmation, but he can't give it. "I don't know, babe. Maybe you should ask your mom."

She laughs bitterly at this. "Yeah, right. What would I say?"

"Tell her what he told you."

She shakes her head emphatically. "I couldn't do that."

Sam nods, not understanding.

"Remember when you said I look like my nephew? My *step-nephew?*"

"Yeah."

Jenna rifles through her purse, digging out her cell phone and searching for the photo. "Did you mean it?"

She passes him the phone, and he looks at the image. "Yeah, I meant it, but—"

"I should ask her straight out."

"Okay."

"No. It's stupid. Why am I getting worked up about this? It's impossible."

"Okay."

For the next few hours, she talks herself in circles. She can convince herself of either point if she talks long enough. Sam wanders back and forth to the living room as he cooks hamburgers for dinner. He sets them on the table without asking her if she's hungry. She talks with her mouth full. He listens.

"I can't go home," Jenna says finally. "I don't know what to do. Can I stay here?"

"Of course."

"Just to sleep."

"Of course."

***

He gives her one of his T-shirts to sleep in. It's fresh from the laundry. When she nestles against his body, the shirt he's wearing smells the same and she realizes that's half of what a person's smell is—their detergent.

He holds her. She lays her head on his chest and his chin rests on the top of her head. They don't talk but she knows he's awake because he kisses her hair from time to time. She can see his alarm clock and watches the minutes scroll past as her neck begins to ache. She doesn't want to be rude, so she stays in this position until her whole left side feels numb, except for a current shooting up her arm.

Jenna tries to remember the first time she met Bill. He would have come to the house to pick her mother up for a date. Or they might have all met him out somewhere. A restaurant, the park. She wants to remember her mother's face in focus, search for signs of deceit. But she can't remember. It was too long ago.

Finally, she slides her head to her own pillow, and Sam shifts onto his side and seems to fall right to sleep.

She can remember the wedding because the event was something she knew was important while it was happening. Her mother looked beautiful in an off-white lace dress that fell at the knee. She and Julie wore pink. Jenna didn't put up a fight about it. Her grandfather had died that summer, that's why Grammy hadn't been there. As Bill offered his vows, it felt like he was giving them to Julie and Jenna, too. And Billy. To all of them becoming a family.

Sam's body obstructs her view of the clock. She lifts her head occasionally to confirm that although time seems to be standing still, the night is indeed flying by. Even though he's asleep and she isn't, she doesn't feel angry at him the way she used to feel on the rare nights Julie fell asleep before her. Before Billy left for college, they shared a room and drifted off at the same time each night, still whispering to each other across the room. It was like one lifelong conversation, persisting after they'd stopped having much to say to each other during the day. In the morning, Jenna could never quite remember what they'd talked about.

She doesn't begrudge Sam his peace, though. She looks at his face up close in the darkness. He has long eyelashes, the kind that almost seem like a waste on a man. They're not all the same color; here and there a blond one is mixed in. His smile lines disappear when he sleeps, and she misses them.

***

In the morning, Jenna wakes to the smell of coffee and is surprised to find she did fall asleep. Sam has put her cell phone on the pillow beside her. It's blinking with a message.

Jenna sits up and yawns. She reaches for her phone and checks voicemail.

Sam comes to the doorway. "Morning sleepyhead. Coffee?"

Jenna opens her mouth to answer when she hears Julie's voice.

"Jenna, where are you? I'm at the hospital with Bill. Oh, God, I can't do this alone! Where are you?"

Chapter Seven

Jenna insists on going to the hospital alone. She pulls on her jeans, pushes on a headband, and tears down the front steps while Sam is still stammering in his boxers. In the car, she runs her tongue along her teeth and wonders vaguely whether she has gum. At a red light, she fingers the change in the console but can't remember what she's looking for. The trees in the park have dropped most of their leaves. They seem unembarrassed by their nakedness, their golden leaves scattered around them like discarded dresses. Jenna tests the car's heater. It blows cool air on her and she quickly switches it off, shivering.

Jenna's wearing Sam's T-shirt when she walks through the automatic doors and finds Julie sitting on the floor in the entryway against the wall. Julie's holding her head, but she looks up when the doors open, and Jenna doesn't have to ask her a thing. She knows.

Jenna crouches in front of her sister and wraps Julie in her arms. Julie sobs and they both ignore the traffic of strangers walking past them.

"Where were you?" Julie cries angrily, pounding a weak fist against Jenna's shoulder. "It was your night."

This knocks the wind out of Jenna. She pulls back. She had left without telling anyone.

Julie gets to her feet, leaving Jenna huddled on the floor, hugging her sides. "I haven't been able to get a hold of Mom. She's flying in today."

Jenna nods slowly. "I'll call her." She stands and pats her pockets until she remembers her phone is in her car.

Julie follows her to the parking lot. "UNH, huh?"

Jenna looks down at her chest. She smells Sam's smell and feels the shame wash over her. "I'm sorry, Julie. I don't know what I was thinking. I wasn't, I wasn't—" She struggles to find words. "Myself?"

"It's okay." Julie sighs. "I shouldn't have said it like that. You couldn't have done anything. He just. He fell asleep." She smiles and starts to cry again.

Jenna hugs her and leads her to the passenger's side of the car where she can sit down.

Julie's legs hang out of the car as she gulps and wipes her nose with the sleeve of her shirt. She presses her hands against her thighs and hangs her head. "You weren't there," Julie blubbers. "I was all alone and he wouldn't wake up!"

The cold pavement sends a dull ache through the knees of Jenna's jeans. She holds Julie's forearms. "I'm sorry," Jenna says again, loud, clear, and heartfelt.

Julie pushes Jenna's hair out of her eyes and nods. She lifts Jenna's headband and sets it in her lap. She runs her fingers down both sides of Jenna's hair, flattening it against her scalp. Julie licks her palm and smooths Jenna's bangs away from her face, replacing the headband.

"Better?" Jenna asks.

Julie shrugs and reaches to pull the car door shut, forcing Jenna to move.

Jenna walks back to the driver's side and finds her cell phone in her seat. She pulls her door closed against the chilly air and the sisters sit together in silence. Jenna holds the phone on her lap, imagining how she will say it, what words she will give her mother when she tells her Bill is gone.

***

When Jenna's mother arrives, the three of them are ushered into a room with Bill. He lies on a gurney with a sheet pulled up to his shoulders, looking about as gray as always. Barbara fusses with the sheet, lifting his arms free and tucking it under his armpits. She sits beside him, holding his hand and whispering close to his face. Julie sits by the door, sniffling. Jenna splits the difference, standing somewhere between them, waiting.

Barbara kisses Bill's forehead and moves to wipe the lipstick mark off with her thumb but decides to leave it there. She turns, sees Julie crying and goes to her with her arms open. Together, they leave the room.

Jenna takes a step towards Bill. She reaches for him, for the hand that touched her face to express his pride and worry and love. And possession. "You're mine," she murmurs, as if she's testing out a theory. The room answers her with silence. She strokes the top of his hand lightly with her fingers. She hears Julie wail out in the hallway and it pulls her to the door, away from this man.

Her father.

***

At home, Jenna's mother sits in Bill's chair with Norman curled at her feet, dozing and looking bored. Julie slouches on the couch, looking out the window while Jenna hovers in the doorway, with the phone in her hand.

It falls on Jenna to make the phone calls. When she tells Billy, he's calm. He assures her he will catch a flight the next day, and then he asks to speak with their mother. Jenna hears his deep voice through the receiver pressed to her mother's ear. Even though she can't hear what he's saying, it feels like comfort. Her mother nods with her eyes closed. Jenna wonders if this is the kind of doctor he'll be.

Bill Jr. answers his cell phone in the middle of the class he's teaching. He cries openly and, as far as Jenna can tell, right in front of his students. He says he'd known the call was coming any day now; he felt it. He sounds almost relieved. He says he will drive down in the morning with Annie and Lucas.

The three of them pore over photo albums, choosing pictures for the funeral home. When she looks back on these days, Jenna will remember this as the only part of the funeral formality that isn't completely barbaric. It manages to feel personal and authentic, unlike the later, public display where their pain must either be falsely hidden or shown in a way that feels more like a performance of grief instead of an experience of grief.

Soon, the well-meaning friends and neighbors will descend upon them with casseroles and baskets of flowers. There will be lists and itineraries and concerns about wardrobe. They will be busy with the superficial details of Bill's death, of doing what's expected of them. They will detach, examining their loss from the outside. It will be days before they have another chance to feel the loss the way it's meant to feel. From the inside.

Sitting on the floor with her sister sifting through the images of their childhood, Jenna has a sense that the grief belongs to them. Barbara looks at the pages over their shoulders, contributing her own memories of each photo. For now, the pain is visceral and honest and *theirs*.

Bill dressed up as an M&M for Halloween.

"He couldn't sit down all night, but he didn't care. He wore that costume two years in a row."

The road trip to Virginia to visit Bill's mother.

"Look at Mom's hair."

"It was humid, and the house had no air conditioning."

"She made us bake pies all day."

"I hate rhubarb."

"But it was Bill's favorite."

"It was?"

"Yeah. She died the next winter." Barbara reaches for the album. "That was the last time he saw her."

Last Christmas, Bill sat in his chair and directed the placement of ornaments on the tree.

"He wanted everything to be perfect. He kept saying it was going to be his last. I told him he was being morbid."

"He was depressed."

"He was right."

They cry. A lot. Sometimes they take turns. Sometimes one person's sobs answer another's. They laugh until they cry. They cry out in anger. They sit silently until it suddenly creeps up on them. They hug each other and pass the box of Kleenex around and cry.

When she finds a moment to call Sam, he's quiet. He asks how he can help, and Jenna can't speak because she's crying. She sits on the floor of the bathroom, leaning against the door. He tells her he's sorry, and he wishes he could do something, and he's there. He offers to come over, but Jenna tells him not to. He listens to her cry for several long minutes.

As the sun goes down, Jenna remembers they haven't eaten all day, and she makes grilled cheese sandwiches. In the refrigerator, she finds Bill's cans of ginger ale and rather than leave them as some sort of shrine, she takes out three and carries them into the den. They each pop one open and crash them together in a wordless toast.

That night, before collapsing into bed, Jenna signs online and drafts an email to Liam. She keeps it short and to the point: "My dad is dead." She clicks *Send* without knowing if he will get it, if he will even care, if she will ever hear from him again. She sends it like a message in a bottle, like a smooth stone dropped into a pool, making ripples; like lighting a fuse and waiting, waiting, wondering if it will be a little pop or a boom or nothing, nothing at all.

***

No one has broken the news to Norman. He lies across the front door, waiting. His hopefulness is heartbreaking and, somehow, makes Jenna envious.

She cooks scrambled eggs and bacon, laying the bacon on a paper towel to absorb the grease. She snaps a piece in half and bends to give it to Norman. She doesn't ask him to do a trick first. He wags his tail when he sees her coming and munches it happily.

Jenna hugs him, burying her face in his golden coat. She holds onto the extra rolls of skin around his neck and looks him in the eye. "He's not coming home, buddy."

Norman gapes at her with his tongue out, panting.

Bill taught Norman all his tricks. He could leave a piece of bacon on the edge of the table and tell Norman to leave it, and he would. He'd stare at the bacon until Bill said he could get it. One time, Bill got distracted and left the house. When he came home, Norman was still sitting there, waiting for Bill's permission.

Norman tolerates fewer people these days. He growled at new guests and people he didn't see often. He put up with Lucas. He settled for attention from the rest of the house when Bill went to the hospital. After a few days without him, Norman grew listless. After Bill's last surgery, Jenna snuck him into the hospital. One of the nurses let her in through the service entrance. Norman trotted down the hallway with purpose, as if he knew where he was going. She didn't know how he'd manage when the days became weeks and months and forever. She didn't know how they'd manage.

"Breakfast!" Jenna calls up the stairs.

Julie plops into a chair as Jenna sets her plate in front of her. Her eyes are pink and swollen.

"Did you get any sleep?" Jenna asks.

"Some." Julie rubs her nose.

"Juice?"

"Okay."

Barbara walks into the kitchen wearing her fuzzy blue bathrobe and pink slippers. She wraps Julie in her arms, kissing the top of her head. Then she walks to Jenna, allowing herself to be enveloped.

"Mom," Jenna murmurs. She feels the weight of her mother's head on her shoulder.

After a few moments, Barbara pulls away with a sigh, wiping her eyes. "Who wants coffee?"

They sit at the table, eating and moving food around on their plates, going over the logistics of the days ahead.

"When Bill Jr. gets here, he'll go with me to the funeral home," Barbara says. "To help me with the decisions. I think he'll keep things practical. You're always hearing how they take advantage of grieving families."

The girls nod. Jenna thinks once the *senior* dies, the *junior* is supposed to get dropped. She hates this idea with every fiber of her being. He will always be Bill Jr. to her.

"Besides," Barbara continues, "Bill was his father. If he has any preferences, I'd like to give him the opportunity."

Bill was his father.

"Did Bill ever make any plans?" Jenna asks.

"He didn't care about any of it. Funerals are for the living, that's what he always said."

A tear slides down Julie's face. Jenna puts an arm around her.

"Someone's going to need to pick up Billy from the airport."

"I'll do it," Jenna says. "What time?"

"I think around two o'clock. I'll check. But first, I need a shower."

Julie and Jenna sit alone at the table, leaning into each other. "Is Brad coming over later?" Jenna asks.

"We're in a fight."

"Does he know what happened?"

"I don't care. I wouldn't want him here. This isn't a time for people who are passing through."

"I guess not."

"When is Sam coming over?"

Jenna's eyes slide sideways, and she can see Julie's little smirk.

***

The water pressure is perfect. It thrums through the pipes and pounds on the back of Jenna's neck. She stands beneath the water long after she's done with the soap. Closing her eyes, lifting her face, she loses herself in the void.

She remembers a girl in elementary school whose mother died. Christine McCarthy. She was a year behind Jenna, in Julie's grade. Jenna remembers the day the principal came to tell her. They were lining up after recess, waiting to go back inside. The fifth-grade teacher was giving a lecture on the necessity of wearing hats. The body loses ninety percent of its heat through the head, she told them. Jenna still wonders if this is true. She's always felt her body's temperature is regulated by her feet.

By the time the students got back to class, the news had spread. It was a car accident. Christine's mother was a Girl Scout leader, and nearly everyone seemed to know her. Jenna had spent one day as a Girl Scout and quit before she had to buy the uniform. She never knew Christine or her mother before the accident. During the following decade, any time their paths remotely crossed at school, it was the first thing that came to mind. No one likes to be defined by their tragedies, but Jenna couldn't help herself.

Years later, finding her picture in a yearbook, Jenna thought to herself: *there's Christine, the motherless girl.*

Of course, this was different, Jenna's version of losing a parent. Supposedly, Jenna is grown. She's a legal adult nearly through college. The *biological* sent a sympathy fruit basket with a card that someone wrote his name on. She hardly has the right to feel fatherless.

When the water cools, Jenna reaches to turn it off. She'd rather keep leaning into the spray with her eyes closed, delaying the moment she's forced to step into the rest of her life.

Jenna hears some commotion downstairs as she gets out of the shower. She dresses quickly and hurries down. Bill Jr. and Annie huddle around her mother on the living room couch. She finds Lucas sitting on the floor in the den, patting Norman.

"Norman's sad." Lucas' hand moves slowly across Norman's head.

"Yeah? Did he tell you that?"

Lucas rolls his eyes, as if he's running out of patience with people who insist on treating him like a child. Jenna tries again. "You can tell from his face?"

Lucas nods. "His eyes mostly. And the way he sighs."

Jenna looks at Norman. He does look sad, but she wonders if she's projecting.

"Are you sad?" Lucas asks.

"I am. How about you?" Jenna sits on the floor and twists a finger around one of the curls on Norman's ear.

"Yeah. Mother says it's okay to be sad."

"I think she's right." Jenna puts her hand on his head and looks at those wide, ice-blue eyes. Bill's eyes. Lucas hugs her, patting her back with his little hand. Such a simple gesture of comfort. *How does he know how to do that?*

"Hey."

She turns to see Sam standing behind her.

"Julie let me in," he says. He puts a hand on the back of Jenna's neck and squeezes. She reaches up and places her hand on top of his.

Lucas steps forward and gives Sam's hand one good shake. "I remember you. You brought the balloons." He smiles and sits down again.

"That's me. No balloons today, though." After a moment, he sits on the floor with them.

Norman grumbles, sneering and showing teeth.

"Norman, stop it!" Jenna scolds.

"It's okay." Sam scoots away a little but stays close enough to keep a hand on Jenna's back.

"He's having a bad day," Lucas explains.

"I understand. I hear that's going around."

Lucas nods, solemnly.

Sam looks at his watch.

"Time to go?" Jenna asks.

"Probably."

"Where you going?" Lucas looks up as Jenna and Sam get to their feet.

"Picking up Uncle Billy." Jenna tussles Lucas' hair, then stops with her hand resting on his head. That's what Bill used to do.

In Sam's car, Jenna leans her head back and closes her eyes. She likes the feeling of the car backing out of the drive, taking her away, even if it is for a short time.

Sam's quiet. He doesn't ask her for anything. He just lets her be.

They pull into short-term parking. They have a few minutes before Billy's flight arrives.

"I can't ask her now," Jenna says, as if she's picking up a conversation they'd been having.

"What?"

"If Bill's my dad. If he was. I can't ask her now."

"There will be time later."

Jenna looks at him across the console. It feels like they're at opposite ends of a long tunnel. "We're going to bury him tomorrow." She wonders if he can hear her.

"I know."

Jenna shakes her head angrily. "No, you don't."

Sam takes a breath. "You're right. I don't."

Jenna covers her face, ashamed. She's not angry with Sam. She wants to apologize, but she doesn't trust her voice.

Sam turns away, looking out the windshield. "I've never been here. I don't know the right thing to do or say to make it better, and I know I can't really make it better." He looks at her. "But I want to."

Jenna tries to smile. "Well, that's nice."

"Tell me what to do, and I'll do it. Whatever you need. I give you free reign to be bossy."

"Hold me?" she asks. Sam opens his arms, and she falls into them. He wraps her up tight. "How long do I get to be bossy?"

He seems to think it over. "A week?"

"That's it?"

"Let's see how the week goes. You might get drunk with power."

"I might." Jenna looks at her watch. "You stay here while I go in and find him."

"Deal," he says. Jenna gets out of the car. As she steps up on the curb, he calls to her, "See, you're already getting the hang of this bossy thing."

Jenna nods. She wants to freeze this moment, take a snapshot. Sam's hair is gold in the afternoon light. He leans his head out the window smiling at her—for her. She feels the cool air on her face and in her mouth. It smells like the first day of school. She doesn't want to take the next few steps forward: Picking up her brother and talking funeral talk. She doesn't want to go backward, either. The past two days have been horrifying in many ways.

But this moment, standing in the warmth of the sun and Sam's gaze, this moment is good.

***

Jenna stands at the baggage carousel for Billy's flight watching the suitcases on their slow glide around and around. She doesn't know what Billy's bag looks like and can't grab any of them. She plays a game with herself, guessing which bag might be his. Obviously, the floral suitcase is off the list and the military style duffle bag. She is deciding between two similar looking black suitcases when one of them is grabbed by an older man. The number of bags on the carousel dwindles. She wonders if Billy made his flight.

She heads toward the escalator. She couldn't have missed him. The Manchester Airport is the smallest one she's ever seen. There are only five baggage carousels, all to the left of the escalator, the ticket counters are to the right. All the gates are upstairs—all sixteen of them.

At the bottom of the escalator, she spots him. He's animated, chatting with a man who looks about his age and is standing two steps above him. He's not paying attention and appears to float toward her without having made the decision to do so. Jenna finds herself worrying he won't know when to step off.

But he does. "Hey, sprout!" He doesn't bother introducing his companion. They shake hands and clap each other on the shoulder before the other man rushes off.

"You made a friend?" Jenna offers.

"Joey Dumas. We went to high school together!" He's grinning at her like this is an amazing stroke of luck. Jenna doesn't remember Joey Dumas.

"Where have you been?"

"We got to talking," Billy says, as if this is an explanation. He puts his hand between Jenna's shoulders, guiding her back toward baggage claim.

The conveyor belt has stopped conveying. Off to the side, under a handwritten sign taped to the wall, Billy finds his suitcase.

The sign says, "Unclaimed Baggage."

***

When it gets dark, they start assigning rooms. Bill Jr. and Annie and Lucas take Jenna's room; she can bunk with Julie. Sam helps Jenna make up the couch in the basement for Billy.

"How are you doing?" Sam asks. He takes the bottom sheet away from her and begins tucking the edges under the couch cushions.

Jenna shakes her head. "It feels unreal. And I keep wanting to call Liam. I mean, whenever I thought about this happening, I always thought he'd be here."

Sam nods.

"I'm glad you're here," Jenna says quickly, "I don't mean—
"

"Jenna, it's okay. You don't need to worry about hurting my feelings. Not today. I understand. He's your best friend. He should be here."

Each of them holds an end of the top sheet as they step away from each other. The sheet catches the air and settles onto the couch.

Jenna sits on the loveseat and watches Sam finish, deciding which end of the couch will be the foot. He pushes a pillow into a pillowcase and punches the middle.

"You know how I feel about you, right?" Jenna asks.

Sam looks up at her. He sets the blanket down, still folded in a rectangle.

"I don't want to say. I don't want to remember it like this. But you know, don't you?"

He sits down beside her. "I think so." Sam smiles and Jenna's fingers trace the lines at the corners of his eyes. "And you know how I feel?"

Jenna's heart races. She uses both hands to press his lips together. "Shh." She presses her mouth against his.

Chapter Eight

Jenna sits in the front pew. Sam sits on her right because she told him to. He holds her hand, and she holds Julie's hand. Julie sits on the other side with her head on their mother's shoulder, sniffling. People get up and speak, and Jenna doesn't listen to any of it. It doesn't matter. Nothing matters.

Julie used the last of the shampoo, so Jenna had to rummage through the drawer of little hotel shampoo bottles her mother collects from all her business trips. Now Jenna's hair smells foreign, like someplace she's visiting. It adds to the unreality of the day.

There's a casket at the front of the church, and Jenna tries to convince herself Bill is inside. She imagines him in the gray suit her mother chose from the closet, although Jenna can't remember him ever wearing it. She tries to remember the last time she saw him wear a suit, and all she can come up with is the light blue suit jacket and navy pants he wore to his retirement party. But that was years ago.

Bill Jr. gets up and stands behind the podium. She can't tell what he's saying—her own personal soundtrack presses at her temples, a buzzing, nonsensical headache, white noise drowning out the organ music as soon as they walked into the church. "Amazing Grace." A lump had started to form in her throat and then, somehow, the music was switched off. It was as if she was plunged into the deep end of a pool. She sits at the bottom watching everything going on mutely beyond the water's surface. She sees Bill Jr. smiling, the crowd in the pews answering with a collective laugh that makes her angry. He looks like Bill did when she first met him. When she was five, being introduced to her father like he was a stranger. Maybe.

She searches Bill Jr.'s face for some hint of her own. But then he bows and returns to his seat, grasping her mother's hand in the aisle before he sits down.

It ends quickly after that. Or it seems to, everything blurring together, some things slowed down, and others sped up. They stand and gather their belongings, and Sam helps her with her coat. Walking down the center aisle, following the casket, Jenna feels eyes on her. Everyone in the church is gawking at the mourners. She tries to let the passing faces become a blur, but she sees Liam in one of the back rows.

***

The grass is brown and stiff with frost. It offers slight resistance, crunching beneath Jenna's step. She wonders whether a grave can be dug when the ground is so cold, but as she approaches the casket, she sees a pile of black dirt off to the side. Waiting.

They huddle under a tent as it drizzles. It's not a full rain, but the crowd has gotten smaller. Some guests have left already, offering their condolences at the church, pointing to the sky. Some are waiting in their cars and will meet them back at the house. Sam drove through a red light in the chain of grieving cars, and Jenna hoped drivers with green lights understood his headlights weren't only about the weather.

Julie stopped crying. She looks exhausted, slack faced and slouching, staring at the ground. Billy has an arm around their mother. The priest speaks briefly, and Jenna wonders if he's always so concise or whether he's eager to get out of the miserable weather. As cold as it is, Jenna prefers it to a sunny day. Sam holds her hand.

As they lower the casket into the ground, Barbara whimpers. At first, Jenna thinks the noise is coming from Julie. She turns to look and sees her sister is equally bewildered. Billy pulls their mother closer, and the wail is muffled against his chest.

By now, everyone but the immediate family has left quietly, returning to the parking lot. Nine of them remain, including Sam. Each of them steps forward to grab a handful of dirt. It's so cold it feels as if it's burning Jenna's hand. It's a relief to let it go, listening to the larger clumps beat against the casket's surface.

They walk away before the grave has been shoveled in and closed forever. They walk away slowly.

***

Liam's standing beneath a leafless tree, rubbing his arms. Jenna lets go of Sam's hand.

"I'll go warm up the car," he says.

Jenna nods. She steps off the path and under the partial shelter of tree branches. She looks at Liam without saying hello.

He takes a breath. "I'm so sorry about your dad."

Jenna nods, her jaw tight, her eyes on the ground. She has nothing more to offer. She can hear the scraping of leaves blowing across the pavement. She waits.

"I've been a complete ass," Liam says at last.

She sighs. "Well, yeah."

"Is it a total cop-out to plead insanity?"

"I don't know."

"Okay." Liam digs the toe of his shoe into the dirt.

"Was it temporary insanity?"

"What do you mean?"

"Are you better?"

"Oh, yeah. For a while now."

"A while?"

Liam flinches. "I should have called. I didn't know what to say."

Jenna nods slowly.

"It was awful, what I said. I understand if you're still mad."

"I don't have the energy to be mad."

A raindrop swells at the tip of a branch and falls noiselessly against the wool of Liam's sleeve. "I'd like to be here for you like I should have been all along."

Jenna squints toward the parking lot. "I have to go. They won't leave without me." She means the waiting cars.

"Oh."

"You coming?"

***

Sam parks on the side of the road, behind another car. The driveway is already full. "Quite a crowd."

"The neighbors will be jealous." Jenna presses her forehead against the cold glass of the passenger's window. She can see figures moving inside the house.

"What can I do?" Sam asks.

"You're doing it." She turns to him and pats his knee.

"Ready?"

She shakes her head as she reaches for the door handle.

They hurry across the lawn and up the front steps. The rain is coming down harder, but Jenna doesn't think to cover her head. She pulls open the front door, the noisy inside chatter competing with the hiss of rain on the pavement. It's already November, and still no one has bothered to change the screens for the storm windows on the outer door. Raindrops are gathered in the little squares of the metal screen, reminding Jenna of rained-on spider webs.

Inside, Sam takes her coat. She feels the weight slide off her shoulders, and she turns to him, finding the calm in his eyes, measuring the moment before she falls back into the funeral chaos.

Sam touches a raindrop on the tip of her nose.

"Jenna Marie!"

Jenna turns and is swept into the arms of an older woman with a large bosom. She can't see her face, but the woman smells like lilies of the valley, and she feels like home.

"Grammy," Jenna sighs, leaning into the soft, sturdy body. Her grandmother's hair is different. It's shorter and grayer. They haven't seen each other in years, but it's still a familiar relief to be held in these arms. "I didn't see you at the church."

"Oh, de-ah," she says in her thick Maine accent, "I got lost. I'm not used to city driving. I went around and around for an hour until I decided I may as well come straight to the house and help set things up. Luckily, I hadn't got myself too turned around. I found my way here fine."

"Well, that's good."

Sam returns from hanging up the coats and Jenna introduces them, repeating the part about city driving for their mutual, unspoken amusement. Jenna's grandmother lives in a part of coastal Maine rural enough to make Manchester seem like New York City.

"I'm sorry about your—about Bill." Grammy shakes her head. She's always stumbled over how to refer to Bill. Jenna always assumed it was a generational thing, unaccustomed to divorces and regrouped families. "I haven't seen you girls in ages. When was it you came over to Maine?"

"That summer." Jenna remembers all the times she and Julie visited. Once they got their licenses, they often drove up during the summers. Sometimes they brought friends along, the lure of beachfront property a few hours away from anyone's parents irresistible to teenagers. The last time was the summer right after high school graduation. Jenna went alone. She sat with her grandmother on the low, wooden beach chairs, watching the waves, drinking glass after glass of lemonade from a pitcher. She spoke of her worry for Julie, a senior with no college plans, and of her own anxiety about starting college in the fall. Grammy wore a straw sunbonnet she held against her head in the breeze while she spoke soothingly. She wasn't worried. Each of the girls would find their way, in their own time. It only felt urgent to Jenna because of the impatience of youth. When Jenna was an old lady, these years would feel like a blink.

Still, Jenna worries for Julie and herself, and she can't believe three years have passed already. "I'll come soon."

Grammy nods. "I'm gonna check on the coffee. You go say hey to your Mama. She's over there." Grammy flaps a hand toward the far wall where Jenna's mother is standing. The two women manage to spend the day this way, always on opposite sides of the room. They haven't spoken to each other in over a decade, but they seem to have agreed to share the space without any unpleasantness.

Barbara sits down on the couch in the living room, nodding while a woman in a floral wrap dress holds both of her hands and speaks with a furrowed brow. Jenna doesn't recognize the woman and doesn't feel like interrupting.

Lucas bounds around the corner and launches himself against Jenna. He wraps his arms around her waist and nestles his head against her stomach.

"Hey, buddy," Sam says, leaning against the doorframe with his arms crossed.

Lucas presses his chin against Jenna's hip, looking up at her. "Where's Norman?"

Jenna combs the top of his hair with her fingers. "He doesn't like crowds, so we put him in the basement."

Lucas sticks out his lower lip and scowls. Jenna palms the back of his head. "Can I go play with him? I'm bored."

Jenna looks around the room through the eyes of a five-year-old. "Have you had anything to eat?"

Lucas sighs dramatically and presses his face against Jenna. "Yes," he says, his voice muffled in the fabric of her dress.

Out the window, Jenna sees Liam sitting in his car. He appears to be talking to himself.

"Can you go with him?" she asks Sam. He straightens his posture and nods. "Keep an eye on Norman. He might not be in the best mood."

Jenna doesn't think Norman would ever bite, but in his old age he's gotten a little snippy when he feels cornered. She holds Sam's gaze, trying to express her concern without saying it out loud.

"We'll be fine," Sam says, and Lucas takes his hand, dragging him to the basement stairs.

Jenna slips back out the kitchen door, neglecting to bring her coat. She darts to Liam's car and pulls on the handle. It's locked. She taps on the glass. Frantically, Liam scrambles to unlock the door for her. He seems to consider it a test of their tentatively reconciled friendship. Jenna slides into the passenger seat with damp hair and chattering teeth.

"Jenna, where's your coat?" Liam wriggles out of his and hands it over.

Jenna drapes it over herself, pulling it up under her chin like a blanket. Liam turns the heat on high.

"I wasn't sure you were coming in." She stamps her feet, speeding up her circulation.

"I was feeling a little anxious."

"Meds kicking in?"

He shrugs. "They're kicking." He's literally wringing his hands.

"It's not scary in there. We have deviled eggs."

Liam looks up at her and smiles. "My favorite."

Jenna nods.

Liam looks back at his hands in his lap. "I feel like I'm taking advantage. Getting forgiveness because you're down."

"Not having the energy to be mad isn't the same as forgiveness."

Liam's eyes widen and then quickly relax. He sighs. The rain is coming down in sheets now. Jenna feels like they're going through a car wash. She can't see the house; she can't see the hood.

"I'm kind of afraid of your mom," Liam admits.

"Why?"

"In case she's mad at me."

It takes Jenna a moment to understand. "My mom has no idea we were ever fighting."

"She must have noticed I haven't been around lately."

"Gosh, *she* hasn't been around lately." Jenna catches herself before going on in anger she hadn't been aware of until now. "She doesn't pay attention to stuff like that," she says instead.

"And Julie?"

"Nope."

"Who do you talk to, Jenna?"

Jenna tilts her head, unsure what he means.

"You know, I never understood how sick he was." Liam places his hands on the steering wheel at ten and two. He squeezes it, turning his knuckles white. "I'm sure part of that, a big part, was how caught up I was with myself," he adds quickly. "But you always downplayed it."

Jenna sighs. She leans forward and lowers the heat. "You're right. I did."

Silence swells between them.

"It was hard imagining getting through this day without you," Jenna says finally.

"I'm here."

They look each other in the eye and something unspoken and necessary passes between them. Jenna nods her head once, firmly. Liam nods back, his jaw set, his eyes moist.

"How long are you staying?" Jenna asks.

"As long as you want me. I'm spending the night with some friends from school. I got my job back next semester, so I'll be moving back."

"Wow. Good for you." Jenna does the math. Barely two months.

"So, what's the story with the yummy guy who's been at your side all day?" Liam asks.

Jenna feels her face flush. The music of the rain changes, growing quieter. The house reemerges across the lawn. "Let's go," she says, pushing Liam's coat toward him.

He laughs, turning the car off and following her into the house with his coat over his head. "I'll get it out of you!" he shouts after her.

***

Jenna's mother is happy to see Liam. She gets up from the couch to hug him and asks him several questions in quick succession before getting distracted by newer guests at the door. Jenna shakes hands with a slew of old men, forgetting their names as soon as they're offered. Eventually, Sam coaxes Lucas back upstairs and introductions are made.

Sam's mother makes a brief appearance, bringing along an apple pie she has made without apples. Jenna thanks her, wondering what it means. The younger people settle around the kitchen table. Over the next few hours, Liam devours a dozen deviled eggs. Nobody keeps track of how many brownies Lucas has eaten. Grammy leaves early, citing her long drive back. The girls promise to drive up before it starts snowing, which—that far north—could be any day now. Jenna's mother manages to be in the bathroom for this.

The evening grows darker than the dark day. Lucas is carried upstairs, limp against his father's shoulder. Norman is released from the basement and let into the yard. Someone wearing stilettos has left marks like hole punches in the hardwood floors. You can see where she spent most of her time, shifting her weight, hundreds of tiny circles in a cluster by the mantle, another by the table where the food was laid out.

Jenna's mother crouches and runs her fingers over the dents as if she's reading a message in Braille. She lets the air out of her lungs slowly, shaking her head. "I'm going to bed," she announces and, without another word to anyone, that's what she does.

***

It's been a long day, but Jenna isn't tired. What she wants, more than anything, is to get away from the house. So, after putting the food away, they leave the rest of the mess for the morning. Sam drives. Liam sits in the back seat.

The rain has stopped, but everything is wet and cold. The pavement is slick and dark and could be ice as easily as water. The three of them step carefully through the parking lot.

Inside, the café is small and nearly empty. There are three tables inside the front window with mixed-matched chairs. There are stools along the counter with ripped upholstery. In a corner, there's an old *Miss Pacman* game that's occupied, to Liam's dismay. On a shelf along one wall, there are board games with boxes ripped and wilted with age. They decide to play *Scrabble*.

"Seven tile or nine tile?" Jenna asks.

"I didn't know you could play with nine tiles," Liam says.

"That's how my Grammy taught me to play."

They agree on the nine-tile version.

"So, what's the story with her and your mom?" Liam asks.

Jenna opens the board across the table, making room for the three coffee cups. "I'm not sure anyone knows the whole story. After my Grampy died, there was something with his estate."

"So, it's money?" Sam asks.

"It's never really the money," Liam says.

Jenna hands out the tile holders.

"Can I play? I'm Brian." Brian has left the *Miss Pacman* game to hover over their table. He's quite tall, but scrawny enough to indicate he's probably about fifteen or sixteen. He has shaggy brown hair and round wire glasses. "I'm very good at *Scrabble*. I always win."

Jenna looks at him to see if he's for real. Then she looks down. She feels she's exempt from having to talk to this person. She waits for someone else to tell him to go away.

Brian sits at their table. Jenna looks at Liam and Sam. They both shrug at her.

Jenna passes a tile holder across the table to Brian. They figure out who is going first and pick their tiles. Brian's presence has brought an end to all conversation that isn't about the game.

"You know, I got everyone at my high school to play hacky sack." He's making intense eye contact with Jenna. "I'm the one who started it."

Jenna nods slowly and looks back at her tiles.

Liam starts with a small word and a measly amount of points. He doesn't care. He's the least competitive person Jenna has ever met. Sam gets a pen from the woman behind the counter and keeps track of the scores on a napkin. He plays well, utilizing the double- and triple-word-score squares. Brian always has his word planned far before it's his turn, and he appears irritated by Jenna's long turn-taking. That's fine with Jenna.

She places her tiles slowly. UNIPED.

"What?" Brian asks.

"Uniped," she answers, flatly.

Sam looks dubious.

"It's a word. It's a one-footed person. Or entity."

At her next turn, she adds an S to UNIPED, forming the word SALT for twenty-two points.

"Come on. Unipeds?" Brian folds his arms across his chest. "Use it in a sentence."

"The unipeds went on a picnic," Jenna deadpans.

Sam and Liam nod, turning their attention back to their own tiles. Brian huffs noisily.

Halfway through the game, Brian's in the lead. He giggles through everyone else's turn, bouncing in his seat. Maybe he has a genuine social disorder. Maybe he's autistic, and Jenna shouldn't be annoyed. There is such a fine line between being an annoyance and having a legitimate mental disability. Perhaps Jenna should be proud of him for getting out in the world, spending an evening trying to make friends with a group of strangers. But Jenna buried her father today.

Brian sets his tiles on the board, hooting and slapping his thigh. "Twenty-eight points!" he shouts.

Sam scribbles the information down.

Liam uses his turn to trade tiles. "I have all vowels."

Jenna rearranges her tiles on the rack, hoping something will come to her. Brian hums the *Jeopardy!* song to indicate his impatience. She glares at him, then looks back at her letters.

She shrugs. She starts setting out her tiles, adding a K to Brian's NIGHT to make the word WOOPOVICK, using all her tiles.

She starts counting her points aloud. "Plus fifty for using all my letters."

Brian is out of his chair. "Woopovick? That isn't a word."

Sam covers his mouth with his hand and nods thoughtfully. "Woopovick? Sure."

"Is there a dictionary in here? I challenge." Brian scans the walls and other tables. There is no dictionary. "That is not a word! What does it mean?"

Jenna stares at him blankly.

"You know," Liam says calmly. "Woopovick. Like, melancholy."

Brian sulks for the rest of the game. Jenna wins.

***

Exhausted at last, Jenna lies in the backseat on the way home. Sam and Liam chatter in the front seat like old friends, and she's too tired to worry about what they might be saying to each other; secrets given away or embarrassing anecdotes told.

They drive by Cremeland, the neon lights sweeping across the car windows, a tiny image repeated in each droplet of rain. Jenna wonders who's getting ice cream at night in November. Bill used to take Norman there, each of them getting a soft serve vanilla cone. Bill sat on a picnic bench, holding a cone in each hand. Norman sat happily at his feet, licking up the ice cream. The people behind the counters knew them both by name. They were regulars.

They let Liam out when they arrive at his car, and Jenna sits up to hug him goodbye.

Sam cranes his neck to face her. Jenna looks at her house with dread. "Can I sleep over?"

Sam smiles and turns the key in the ignition. Jenna lies down again.

Chapter Nine

Fred the Baker retired from the commercial business in the late nineties. There was a press conference, and Dunkins locations nationwide gave away free donuts to celebrate his retirement. The real man would pass away to much less fanfare.

On Jenna's first day back at work, her coworkers have trouble maintaining eye contact.

"Sorry about your dad," Molly says.

Jenna struggles with her response. *Thanks? That's okay?* Before she decides what to say, Molly flees to the drive-thru window. It's sort of a relief.

It's easier to help the customers who know nothing about her. They don't feel sorry for her or treat her like she's been caught kissing someone else's boyfriend. They simply order their coffees and ask for extra cream cheese for their bagels.

When Jimmy arrives to take her picture, she's comforted by the familiarity of it. She's more surprised than he is when Molly starts shouting: "Have some respect! Her father recently died!" Jenna isn't sure she sees the connection. She looks around self-consciously, the unwitting center of attention in someone else's outburst.

"I'm going to take a break," Jenna says. As she walks to the door, she's only a few steps behind her so-called stalker. Sam enters the convenience store, holding the door for a sulking Jimmy.

Sam reaches for her, touching the sides of her arms. "You okay?"

"Fine," Jenna says.

Molly and Ashley are clearly staring at them. Sam lowers his hand to Jenna's stomach and begins speaking high-pitched nonsense to the front of her smock. Jenna pulls him out the door, her laughter making visible explosions in the frigid air.

They climb into the back seat of Sam's car. Sam leans forward to start the engine and warm it up. Jenna sinks into her seat, planting her feet against the seat in front of her. She unties her boots and tightens the laces, first one and then the other.

"So, what's it like at home?" Sam asks.

Jenna shrugs. Last night was her first night back since the funeral. She left Sam's house early yesterday morning, feeling guilty. But her mother and Julie were still sleeping and hadn't noticed she'd been gone.

"Mom's flying to Denver this afternoon."

"Already?"

She hears his judgement but doesn't respond. "Julie took pity on Norman and let him sleep in her room."

"We could take him out to the park later."

Jenna reties her second boot and puts her feet on the floor. "A telemarketer called for Bill this morning. I felt this wicked sort of glee telling them he was dead."

Sam pats his thighs, and she puts her head in his lap. "You still haven't talked to your mom." It isn't a question. He knows.

"I'm not going to."

"Ever?"

"I don't think it's true. She would have told us. Especially when he got sick."

"If you're sure."

"I am. I got caught up in thinking my life was suddenly an episode of *The Maury Show: Who's Your Daddy?*"

Sam runs his fingers through her hair, trying to tuck her bangs behind her ears. "Getting close," he says.

Jenna closes her eyes, trying to shut out the practical thoughts of the too-long break she's taking, what she will face when she gets home, the overwhelmingly mysterious shape of the coming days. She gives her full attention to the feeling of Sam's fingertips on her forehead and scalp.

***

Jenna doesn't mind making the long drive alone. Part of her really enjoys the solitude, the heat cranked up along with the Indigo Girls. She prefers the idea of having Grammy to herself. But Julie should have come along. There's no excuse.

Julie had several, of course. Jenna wanted to leave the house too early. Julie was sure she'd get carsick. Someone had to stay with Norman. The bottom line became clear rather quickly: Julie didn't want to go, and no amount of bargaining could get Julie to do something she didn't want to do.

As children, Julie was the one who threw tantrums. She'd fling herself down in the middle of the cereal aisle, screeching and turning purple over her sudden, inexplicable hatred of Cheerios. To get out of the store, their mother would relent and allow Frosted Flakes, which grew soggy in the smallest amount of milk and made Jenna gag. But Jenna would keep this to herself.

In the summer, the highway was clotted with beach goers. Cars crept along for an hour or more by the Hampton tolls and again through Kittery. But today, Jenna flies through the tolls without stopping to throw change, grateful for the E-Z Pass tag on her windshield. Bill gave both the girls accounts last Christmas. Bill's gifts were always practical: Gas cards, windshield scrapers, key chains with alarm buttons. Their mother was more likely to buy the frivolous things: jewelry, silk scarves, ballerina figurines. Every year there was a balance. But this year would be absolutely frivolous, frivolous in every possible way.

Jenna drives over the speed limit the whole trip, traffic thinning out the farther north she travels. She hasn't been to her grandmother's house in the winter since she was five. After the move to Manchester, they had made the trip at Christmas and again for Easter. By then, the snow was so deep Jenna remembers the piles at the end of the driveway over her head. Of course, she was much shorter then.

Those were the only two times she met her grandfather. He died early in the summer, and then Jenna's mother married Bill and somehow the family trips north stopped. It had never occurred to her then to wonder why.

Eventually, when she asked, she was told this was *grown-up stuff*. She doesn't remember how she pieced together it had something to do with her grandfather's will. *Little pitchers have big ears*. After a few years, Grammy rejoined their lives, although it was clearly for the sake of the children. She attended school plays and met the children for dinner at neutral locations. Interactions between mother and daughter were brief and pained.

Jenna gets off the highway and drives up the coast in Boothbay. She's surprised to find most of the shops open, though she doesn't see many shoppers. She spots the familiar green and yellow sign for saltwater taffy, the spinning metal machine in the storefront display. She parks the car and watches the surf through the windshield, cracking her window. The salty wind is too cold to take in. The bitter chill makes her breathless, and she rolls the window back up. A figure in a parka jogs along the beach as gulls swoop in the white winter sky.

It's ironic. Jenna's mother had moved to Manchester to be closer to her parents, but her father had quickly died, and her mother wanted nothing to do with her.

The rest of the drive is quick; Jenna feels certain she could do it blindfolded. The gravel driveway crunches beneath the tires, signaling her arrival. At once, her grandmother is standing at the front door, holding it open in the cold, and Jenna hurries inside.

As usual, the old house is dark inside; heavy drapes at the salt encrusted back windows hold out the bright sun, keeping it cool in the summer and cold in the winter.

Reluctantly, Jenna gives her coat to her grandmother. "Jeez, Grammy, do you have the heat on?"

Grammy mumbles something about oil prices as she hangs the coat in the closet. She pulls a dark gray sweater off a shelf and hands it to Jenna. "Layers."

Somehow, after all these years, the sweater still smells like her grandfather. A memory hits Jenna she didn't know she had. She's sitting on her grandfather's lap as he smokes a cigar, a heavy sweetness in the air all around her. With his other arm, he holds her around the waist as she dives into her Christmas stocking. She remembers falling asleep with the smell in her hair.

Jenna pulls the sweater on quickly and follows her grandmother into the kitchen where the table is set for lunch.

"Would you like me to make some tea?"

Jenna hugs herself, nodding. As her grandmother fills the kettle, she excuses herself to the bathroom.

In contrast to the rest of the house, the bathroom is bright enough to hurt her eyes, all white tile with a porcelain clawfoot tub. There's a window next to the toilet with a view into the neighbor's house and an unfortunate broken shade.

Jenna wonders if her grandmother is really having trouble with her heat bill. Should she ask? And what sort of solution would she propose? This is the kind of thing Jenna's mother should worry about. It's her job. The system has fallen apart.

Jenna runs the water in the sink and is relieved when it gets hot. There's a sliver of soap glued to the edge of the counter with deep grooves like wrinkled flesh. It smells like Ivory.

Grammy is setting the mugs of tea by their plates. "Egg salad," she says, motioning to the sandwiches cut on the diagonal.

Jenna sits down. "Thanks." She wraps her fingers around the mug, imagining the warmth traveling up her arms.

"Too bad Julie couldn't come."

Jenna nods. "You know, nine a.m. is the crack of dawn for Julie."

"I had a job for you two."

"A job?"

"I want you to put stickers on the things of mine you want when I'm gone."

"Gram!"

"They're color-coded. Julie's are pink and yours are orange. I have it written down. That way, there's no confusion."

"Gram, no, that's—" Jenna falters, shaking her head wordlessly.

"It's practical. I'm not going to live forever."

"You are," Jenna says stupidly, unintentionally whining, protesting her grandmother's death like a child stamping her feet.

Her grandmother snorts. "I hope not."

Jenna can't help but laugh at this. She reaches across the table and lays her hand on Grammy's papery soft forearm.

Grammy pats Jenna's hand, smiling. "How is Julie doing anyway?"

Jenna takes her hand back. *Buck up*. "Okay. We've been fighting a lot since I moved home."

"Oh, you shouldn't do that." Grammy scowls. "It was one thing when you were children, but you should be more careful now. A sister is a precious thing."

Jenna tilts her head, her eyebrows knitting together. She takes a breath and lets the words out on the exhale: "And a daughter?"

Grammy looks up from her plate, a spot of mayonnaise on her lip. "Of course, a daughter."

Jenna feels a little surprised she has spoken out loud, and her grandmother has heard her words, acknowledged them. "Do you think you and Mom will ever work things out?" she asks, buoyed by the sense of power.

Grammy sighs. "I pray for it every day."

For some reason, the passivity of this answer angers Jenna. "Have you tried?"

"Jenna." Grammy takes another bite of her sandwich, suggesting the end of the subject.

"I bet she could use her mother right now," Jenna mumbles, taking a sip of her tea. It's bitter without sugar and warms her insides.

"I'm right here where I've always been," Grammy says gently.

"Is it as easy as that?"

"Easy?"

"She's the one who's mad? About Grampy's will?"

"Is that what she says?"

"No. She never talks about tit."

Either the tea or the adrenaline of the conversation makes Jenna feel suddenly hot. "What was it?" she asked. "How did it start?" She never felt allowed to ask these questions before, but she suddenly has an awareness of herself as an adult, a grown person with a right to know the truth about the stories that have shaped her.

"Who can say? It's been a lifetime of trials. Your mother was not an easy child."

Jenna's discouraged by her grandmother's vagueness. For a time, there's nothing but the sound of their slow chewing

Grammy takes a long swallow of her tea, draining the mug and setting it down forcefully, as if she's taken a shot of whisky. "Your mother ran off and got married right after she turned eighteen. We didn't hear from her again until we got Billy's birth announcement about exactly nine months later. Postmarked Ohio." Grammy narrows her eyes, frowns at the memory. "We didn't get to meet our grandson until he was three years old."

"So, you missed both of her weddings."

"I surely did. Wasn't invited to either one."

"I didn't know that."

"Well." Grammy shrugs. "How is she holding up? Your mother."

Jenna sighs. "Hard to say."

"Bill was a good man. I wasn't always sure, but he did right by you girls."

"It's funny. I can't remember the two of you ever being in the same room."

"That's because we met before you were born." Grammy motions to Jenna's plate with a bob of the head, pointing with her chin. "You done?"

Jenna looks down. She has left the crusts behind. "Yeah."

Grammy collects the plates and takes them to the sink. Jenna sits for a moment, confused.

"What do you mean, you met him before we were born?" Jenna gets up and follows her grandmother, setting her mug on the counter.

Grammy is about to turn on the faucet. She looks at Jenna. "I knew his family. He grew up around here. I thought you knew that."

"No."

Grammy turns her attention back to the sink, speaking louder as she rinses the lunch plates. "The Shaws had a summer place over to Boothbay. Bill was up here that summer fixing it up to put on the market. That's how they met."

"What summer?"

"After your grandfather's first heart attack. Your mother came from Ohio to help. To be honest, I always thought it was a pretense. She was having trouble in her marriage and wanted to get away, that's what. She left Billy in Ohio with your father."

"How old was he?"

"Six or seven?" Grammy sets the plates to dry on the dish rack and wipes her hands on a wrinkled dishtowel. "She was footloose and fancy free all summer, that's for sure. Acted like a schoolgirl. She fought with your granddad a lot. I don't see how it helped with his ticker."

"What did they fight about?"

"He thought she needed to get back to her husband and son. She did, at the end of the summer, and they must have patched things up. They had you and your sister that spring and lasted a few more years at least." Grammy pulls a drawer open and hands Jenna a sheet of stickers. "Why don't you get started? I have to make a phone call."

Jenna takes the paper, looking at all the small orange circles. She looks up at her grandmother, feeling helpless and small. "Are you sure you're okay?"

Grammy smiles, reaching out to pat Jenna's cheek. "Oh, silly girl," she says tenderly. "I am an old woman. Besides that, I'm peachy."

Jenna looks back with uncertainty.

"Humor me," Grammy says finally and Jenna nods, eager to be of use.

***

Jenna sits on a floral couch in her grandmother's living room, a sheet of orange stickers on her lap, trying to pretend she's looking around at the objects in the room. She's alone in the room; the pretending is for herself. There are too many things she doesn't want to think about competing for room in her head. They seem to cancel each other out, and she's left staring at the patterned wallpaper, a black and white picture of a prairie family in a covered wagon repeated over and over around the room, making her dizzy.

Her mother had known Bill before she and her sister were born. Jenna does the math on her fingers several times. She counts from August to April. It comes to eight months every single time.

Could her grandmother be so naïve as to not realize the bomb she just dropped?

Grammy. An old woman who can't pay her oil bill. She's going to die someday, maybe soon, and Jenna will go through the house, collecting objects with orange stickers.

She thinks of Bill in the hospital, talking about her mother's long hair. Pictures of her mother with hair falling past her shoulders. She cut it short before the girls were born, while she was pregnant.

Jenna sticks out her jaw and blows her bangs up off her forehead. She fingers the letter she's put in her pocket, still in its envelope, folded into a small square. *Results Abnormal*. She doesn't want to think about that, either.

After the divorce, they moved to New Hampshire. Jenna always assumed it was to be near their grandparents. But then, why not move to Maine? Why move three hours away?

Bill lived in Manchester.

Jenna tucks an orange sticker under the edge of the coffee table. It's dark wood and oval. In her apartment with Liam, they had used a plywood board across two plastic crates. They'd covered it with a sheet.

She has no memories of living in Ohio. The girls were only five when their parents split up; Billy was twelve. But she does remember the little house on Essex Street where the four of them had lived for less than a year before they moved to the bigger house on the east side of the river. Bill's house. Where her mother married Bill in the back yard. Where she lives now.

It had happened so quickly. He'd been willing to love them all, right from the beginning.

She sticks a circle onto the knee of her jeans.

"You're mine." That's what he'd said.

***

When Grammy finishes with her phone call, she comes into the room in a tizzy. They're expecting freezing rain in the evening, making the drive back potentially hazardous. They spend the rest of the afternoon listening to the radio. They play cards and Grammy wins every game of *Rummy*. Jenna makes up for it when they play checkers. Grammy keeps leaving her red plastic game pieces in a position to be double jumped. She hushes Jenna when the weather updates come on.

Over dinner, Grammy convinces Jenna to stay the night. After they eat, Jenna helps her grandmother make an apple pie. Mostly, she does the measuring while Grammy juggles the ingredients. Every time Jenna has tried to make a pie crust, it crumbles and tears. Her grandmother rolls it out expertly, her knobby, arthritic fingers transformed into instruments of grace.

When Grammy yawns for the third time, they decide to call it a night. Jenna carries the sheets upstairs to make the bed, noting the thick coating of dust on the banister. Grammy's bedroom is on the first floor, and Jenna suspects she must not use the stairs anymore.

She gets under the covers, but it's too early to sleep so she calls Liam, catching him up on all she hasn't told him about Bill and what her grandmother told her today. She imagines he will be the voice of reason, bringing her back to the sensible humdrum of reality. That's his job.

"Tell me it's impossible," she says, finally.

Liam is silent.

"What?"

"I'm wondering how you can still have any doubts."

Jenna sits up, hugging her knees. She moves her feet against the sheets and is disappointed with the inadequacy of friction. "Why wouldn't my mother have told us? After she left my father. My, you know, the other Bill. The first Bill."

"God, *the biological*. How ironic."

"I know. It's insane. But if she cheated on her husband, I mean, that's awful, but—" She gestures uselessly in the dark room. "Who cares? Why would she keep it a secret still? After they divorced? And he was such a deadbeat anyway."

"Sometimes lies snowball."

"But when he was dying?"

"It's awful."

"I still don't believe it."

"What more proof do you need? Ask your mother."

Jenna lays back, pulling the blanket under her chin. The thought of talking to her mother makes her queasy. "I can't"

"You can't?"

Barbara would never let herself be caught in a lie. She'd deny it, and Jenna would be the villain for thinking such a thing could be true. For speaking of this when Bill's loss was still new and hard to bear. "Not until I'm sure."

"What will make you sure? I mean, it's too late to do a paternity test."

"I don't know yet."

"I'm sorry, Jenna." They're quiet together for a moment. "Hey, I thought of the bright side."

"Oh, yeah?"

"Your name. You've always hated Smiley. But you're really a Shaw. Jenna Shaw."

"Maybe." There are in fact many reasons to delight in Bill being her real father. But, if it's true, the real question becomes: Who is her mother?

Who the hell is she?

Chapter Ten

Two days later, Jenna pulls onto the side of a road in Vermont, waiting. Sam offered to come along, but she needs to do this by herself. The first time she tried to call Bill Jr., Sam wondered aloud, "Are Buddhists allowed to have cell phones?"

"He's not Amish." Jenna laughed about that for minutes; deep belly laughs bringing tears to her eyes. Sam shrugged and smiled, flashing those familiar starbursts, amused to be the butt of her joke. She'd had to hang up and try making the call again later.

She hadn't laughed like that since Bill died. It was a sign she would eventually feel like herself again, which also felt wrong somehow. Disloyal.

At last, she sees Bill Jr. come out from behind the line of trees. He walks with Lucas on his shoulders across the field toward Jenna.

Jenna gets out of her car. It's a bright day, but cold. She zips up her parka and walks toward them. She has never visited the commune before this, but she's seen pictures and feels somewhat prepared.

The dirt path winds through the woods, behind the large main house where the members of the commune prepare most of their meals, have a school room for the children, and gather to pray. It's about a mile and a half to their mini barn—a large, beige shed you'd find for sale at Home Depot. They pass several of these along the way, the homes of other members. The sheds painted with peach, orange, or teal are used as shrines.

"You should see these gardens in the spring," Bill Jr. says.

Jenna nods, focused on her breathing as the path ahead grows steep.

"When it snows, I can sled to school," Lucas chirps eagerly, bouncing up the hill.

Jenna leans against a tree, with a hand on her hip.

"Almost there," Bill Jr. says over his shoulder, not winded at all.

At the top of the hill, there's a large field with a few more sheds scattered at twenty-foot intervals. An outhouse stands at the edge of the clearing. Jenna's thankful she made the stop at the gas station restroom. She never went camping as a kid, a city girl growing up in New Hampshire.

Annie's standing outside one of the mini barns, bent over a Rubbermaid container, one of those thirty-gallon tubs Jenna uses to hold her shoes. Annie straightens when she sees them, waving with one arm and holding a hot plate in the other. Jenna hugs her at the entrance, a sliding glass door, sneaking a peek into the bin. Inside, she sees pots and pans, kitchen utensils and assorted carpentry tools.

Besides the glass door, the shed has no windows. Inside, in the far corner, a single floor lamp is the only other source of light. Jenna's surprised they have electricity. She tries to remember if she saw power lines.

A double bed on a frame takes up another corner of the room. The three of them sleep there together. The plan is at some point, they will get another smaller shed to give Lucas his own room. A few years ago, Annie came into some money when a relative died. They had talked about the possibility of buying a house, but they prayed about it and ultimately decided to give the money to the commune.

Over the years, Jenna has wondered if the commune is a cult, where exactly to draw the fine line. Lucas is sweet and clever and seems happy. In the end, Jenna finds that to be the only meaningful measurement.

It's sort of like visiting another country. Jenna takes a seat on one of the two folding chairs at the metal card table. Bill Jr. sits across from her, and Lucas scrambles eagerly onto his lap.

Annie plugs in the hot plate. On a plastic shelving unit, there are a few bowls and mugs, plastic containers of something that looks like granola, and several gallons of water.

"Did you have school today, Lucas?" Jenna asks, stalling.

Lucas giggles, burying his face in his hands.

Jenna smiles, waiting patiently for the punchline.

"I have a new name."

"A new name?"

Lucas nods, grinning. He hops down and steps toward Jenna. "I'm Ashoka."

"Ashoka?" Jenna squints, unsure of the pronunciation.

"It's the name of a great king," Lucas says proudly.

"Oh." Jenna looks up at Bill Jr. "We aren't calling him Lucas anymore?"

"We'd prefer not," he says simply.

"Oh." Jenna looks back at her beaming nephew and feels inconsolable grief. Her eyes fill with tears.

Annie sets two mugs on the table. "We have to go for a walk," she says, touching Jenna's shoulder lightly. She steers her son outside as Jenna blinks and clears her throat.

Over the phone, Jenna had told Bill Jr. only that she wanted to talk to him in private. He leans back in his chair now, waiting.

"It's so quiet here," Jenna manages.

"Yes. Most of us are down at the main house."

Jenna nods. "So." She leans forward, her elbows on the table, her hands clasped. "Looks like I may be getting a new name myself."

"Oh?"

"I think Bill might have been my real father."

"Ah." He doesn't seem surprised, but she has never seen him surprised.

"Did Bill ever say anything to you about it?"

"No." He takes a sip from his mug. "What makes you think this?"

"Something he said when he was sick."

Bill Jr. nods. "Have you asked your mother?"

"No."

He nods again, sitting quietly. He doesn't ask for an explanation.

Jenna investigates the murky liquid in her mug. There are flakes of debris floating in it like fish food.

"How can I help you?" he asks, and Jenna is thrown, overwhelmed by such simple generosity.

"I want to get a DNA test to see if we're related. You and I."

Bill Jr. raises his eyebrows at her.

"There's a place in Burlington. We'd go, and they'd take our blood and get back to us. I made an appointment in the hope you'd say yes." Jenna holds her breath.

"Yes." Bill Jr. smiles at her. "If this is what you want to do, of course I say yes."

Jenna closes her eyes, pressing her hands against her forehead with relief.

***

Jenna sits on the foot of Sam's bed, crossing her legs and tucking her feet under her, while he brushes his teeth. She talks rapidly about the lab and the commune and the drive to Vermont and back. Her narrative is not linear; she goes back and forth as she remembers details she left out the first time.

Sam sets his toothbrush in the holder and walks toward her. He strokes the band-aid at her inner elbow. "You've gotten so brave," he says, kissing the top of her head.

And then, she's gone, dissolving into tears.

"Oh, babe." Sam sits beside her, wrapping his arms around her. "Long day, huh?"

Jenna shakes her head. "There's something else."

"What?"

Jenna finds the piece of paper she's been carrying around for days. She unfolds it and hands it over.

Sam takes the page and squints down at it. He looks up at her. "What does this mean? Results abnormal?"

"It's my annual pap test. It means they found something weird, and I have to go back for more tests."

"Okay. More tests. For?"

"Cancer. Cervical cancer."

"Okay." Jenna can tell he's trying not to look concerned.

"It's probably nothing," she says, wiping her cheeks.

Sam hands the letter back. "How worried are you?"

"You know, for years I've been writing cervical cancer on every medical history chart I ever fill out. That's how my grandmother died. The *biological's* mother." She does finger quotes as she spits out the word. "I was scared when I got the letter, like I'd been waiting for it. But I shouldn't have been."

Jenna thinks of the last time she saw that grandmother. She and Julie were fourteen, spending their summer week in Ohio. The *biological* had taken them to the hospital to see her. She was frail and bald from chemotherapy. Her terror-filled eyes did all her communicating. Her son held one of her hands and motioned to the girls to take the other. Julie had stepped back and Jenna had hesitated. In the pre-internet nineties, the closest she'd ever seen to something like this was old photographs in history class, victims of famine and war.

Come to think of it, this is probably why Julie hates hospitals. Jenna has pushed the memory down so far; it's only now coming back to her. She can't remember whether she'd taken the old woman's hand. She hopes she did.

"I mean, I'm still scared, but I don't know. I'm so...mad."

"Shit, Jenna, I'm glad to hear it. You should be mad."

Jenna lies back on the bed with a groan. Sam lies next to her, pulling her close, making spoons.

"When is your appointment?"

"Tomorrow."

"I'll go with you," he says, and she doesn't have to ask if he means it.

***

Sam takes the morning off so he can sit in the waiting room while Jenna has her feet in stirrups, staring at a speckled ceiling. Surprisingly, her doctor has referred her to a rather upscale women's health center with a lavish hotel-inspired waiting room. There's a table set with a thermos of hot water, teabags, and a bowl of honey with a little silver spoon. Someone in the office has an apparent affection for panda bears; there are stained glass windows with scenes of pandas munching on bamboo, panda shaped pamphlet holders on the front desk, a stuffed panda sitting in a corner chair. The only other couple in the room is a prematurely balding man and his very pregnant wife. They both have a slight sheen on their foreheads despite the gentle whir of the air conditioner. It's colder inside than out.

The examining room is warmer though, by some magic Jenna has never experienced before. *So, this is how the other half lives.*

Jenna's eyes wander. A shelving unit against the wall has various white plastic baskets with labels. *Laminarian inserter. Endocervical speculum. Lateral vaginal retractor.* Words she doesn't recognize are somewhat ominous for the mystery of what pain they might inflict, words like *tischler* or *tenaculum.* She can't decide if she's more intimidated by these or by words she does know. One basket is labeled scissors.

Jenna's gynecologist has a blonde bob and wears a white coat with her name embroidered in bright blue thread over her left breast. Dr. Maria Bartlett.

"You're going to feel a little discomfort," she says.

Jenna hates that word. Dr. Bartlett is removing a piece of Jenna's cervix to test it for cancer. It will hurt like a motherfucker, and she wishes they could be honest about that.

At one point, Jenna breathes in sharply, and the assistant says, "Breathe in through your nose and out your mouth."

Jenna wants to stab her with the scissors. She says nothing and focuses on breathing however the hell she wants.

It does hurt, but it's over quickly. Sam takes her back to his apartment where she curls up on the couch. He sits across from her on the coffee table, holding out a glass of water and two tablets of Ibuprofen. She takes them gratefully. The cramping comes in waves and makes her nauseous.

"Can I get you anything else?" Sam asks.

Jenna shakes her head, pulling the blanket under her chin and leaning her head on a throw pillow.

"I'll bring home dinner."

Jenna shoots a warning look.

"We don't have to talk about that now," he amends.

She nods and closes her eyes.

***

Jenna wakes up a few hours later. Oprah's audience is screeching about free gifts like converts at a revival meeting. She's not sure if that woke her or the cramps, but now that's she's awake, they refuse to be ignored. They contract sharply in rhythm with her pulse. She takes more Ibuprofen, not pausing to count the hours since her last dose. She wants to sleep through this day, and she pads into Sam's bathroom, opening his medicine cabinet with the hope of an over-the-counter sleep aid.

Inside, she finds stacks of individually wrapped bars of soap, no doubt the result of a sale at Costco. She finds several orange prescription bottles, one for Valium that she sets aside. She reads the labels, not recognizing most of the names. Then she finds one that's familiar: Zoloft.

Jenna takes one Valium and carries the bottle of Zoloft to the couch. There, she huddles under the blanket again and contemplates the label from the pharmacy. The prescription was filled a few weeks ago and there are two refills available before the end of the year.

The phone rings twice. Jenna scowls at the machine, at Sam's sweet voice on the outgoing message.

"Jenna, you awake?" It's Sam. "I thought I'd pick up fried chicken. Sound good?" He waits for her to pick up, hums a bit. "Speak now or forever hold your peace." Another pause. "Okay babe, I'll be home soon."

The incongruity of the familiar and the foreign makes Jenna's head hurt. She looks back and forth between the blinking red light of the answering machine and the bottle in her hand.

Somehow, she manages to fall asleep again. When she wakes, Sam's sitting on the coffee table, looking at her with an expression she hasn't seen before. Is he hurt? Is he angry? The edges of the room are fuzzy. Sam's skin seems to be hanging on his face. She follows his gaze to her lap where the bottle of pills has rolled out of her sleepy hand. It comes back to her then, his secret. She smells the chicken, and her mouth waters as her stomach tightens.

Sam snatches the bottle and stands up. He stomps into the bathroom and Jenna hears the medicine cabinet open and slam shut. He walks back into the room and stands in front of her, breathing hard. He sits on the table again and rubs the top of his head until his hair is standing up crazily. He sighs.

"Are you okay?" he asks.

Jenna nods, wide-eyed and confused. She isn't totally awake yet and feels a vague sense of shame competing with an anger she isn't sure she has a right to. Maybe for the first time since they've met, she can't read him at all, and it has set her completely adrift.

"Why?" This is all she can manage.

"I have obsessive compulsive disorder," he says without looking at her.

Jenna thinks again of all that soap. The hand washing. The neatness. "No." she says.

Sam looks up at her then. "I do," he says, seemingly unprepared to have to convince her it's true.

Jenna shakes her head. "That's not what I meant. "She tries again. "Why didn't you tell me?"

He shrugs.

"I tell you everything," Jenna says, her voice trembling. "I don't tell anyone everything."

"I know." Sam looks down again. He taps his feet against the bottom edge of the couch. For a long time, that's the only sound in the room.

"I've gone and told you everything and you're keeping me out?" Jenna says finally. "Where does that leave me?" she demands, in a sudden panic. She's reasonably sure she knows exactly where it leaves her: alone, hanging off the edge of a cliff that, only moments ago, had been solid ground. "I don't know if I like a movie until you see it and we talk about it." This feels related somehow.

"The movie version of *here, smell this.*"

"It's not funny."

Sam nods. Neither speaks for a while. Jenna finally emerges from the fogginess of her drug-induced sleep.

"Why?" she asks again.

"You made fun of Liam for taking medication," Sam says quietly.

"No, I didn't." Jenna sits up straighter. "I did?"

Sam nods glumly.

"But I was *mad* at Liam. I was venting."

He shrugs.

Jenna covers her face, remembering the conversation he's referring to. She had done an impersonation of Liam in a panic, taking a pill and becoming catatonic. They laughed then. Hadn't they?

"That's a cop-out," she says.

"What?"

"I make one stupid joke, and you shut me out? What else are you keeping from me?"

"Nothing. I mean, I don't know."

"You don't know?"

"God Jenna, we never promised to tell each other everything."

This stuns Jenna into silence. He's right. She begins folding the blanket. "I guess

I thought it was supposed to go both ways."

Sam shrugs.

"I have to go," she says. She finds her keys on the kitchen table. He doesn't try to stop her.

She starts her car and sits in the driveway as it dawns on her she shouldn't be driving. Again, Jenna pictures herself making fun of Liam. She turns off the engine and goes back into the house.

Sam's still sitting on the coffee table. He looks up at her when she walks in.

"I took some of your valium," she says.

Sam nods. "Do you want me to drive you home?"

Jenna walks to the couch and sits down. "No." She grabs his arm, shakes it. "I'm sorry."

"Okay," he says and allows her to pull him into a hug. "I'm sorry too. I didn't want to be another crazy person in your life."

"Oh, what's one more?" Jenna laughs.

Sam pulls back, frowning.

She takes his hands. "Sam, you're the sanest thing in my life. You make more sense to me than anyone I've ever known."

"Yeah?"

"Yeah." Jenna rubs his hair with her palm, smoothing it back in place. "I need you to tell me stuff. I want to be on your team."

Sam raises his eyebrows. "My team?"

"Yeah. You're on my team, right?"

"I am."

"So, tell me everything."

He leans in close to her and lowers his voice. "Well, I'm a little bit crazy."

"We're all a little bit crazy."

***

Jenna meets Liam for coffee near campus.

He's staying with friends for now, not-so-secretly hoping he and Jenna will get an apartment together for the spring semester. He's started seeing Dr. Mackie again, getting his support system in place before he starts teaching again in January.

Jenna gets there first, orders her coffee and hovers by the doorway, unwilling to commit to a table choice. When he arrives, she's struck by how good he looks. He's wearing a charcoal peacoat and a pumpkin-colored scarf wrapped back and forth around his neck, just so. His cheeks are rosy from the cold and remind her of old-fashioned cartoons of happy children. He gets coffee and a large chocolate chip cookie for them to share.

"How was therapy?" Jenna asks as they settle into a secluded corner of the cafe.

"It's nice. It feels very decadent to talk about yourself and be totally self-absorbed for an hour a week." Liam shrugs off his coat and unwinds his scarf.

"I'm glad you're enjoying it."

"And there's this cute guy I've seen in the waiting room two times already. Today I made crazy flirty eye contact with him. I stared at him, thinking: 'I want to have sex with you.' The only way I can talk to him is telepathically, so I have to really work it."

"Wow," Jenna laughs. "Sounds serious."

"And how are things going with the boy? Still like him?"

"I do," Jenna says.

"Me too." Liam nods, as if agreeing with himself. "He seems to be making you happy."

"He does." Jenna hears the sappiness in her voice and shakes her head. "When I really think about it, it's kind of terrifying."

"Good."

"Good?"

Liam nods emphatically. "It's about time you let a boy get close enough to scare the shit out of you."

Jenna laughs. Outside the window, a gust of wind pushes a crumpled bit of newspaper down the sidewalk. Jenna still hasn't taken off her coat. She hunches over her steaming beverage.

"You're starting back next semester, right?" Liam asks, breaking off a bite of cookie.

"That was the plan," Jenna says.

"Was?"

"I don't quite feel capable of making any decisions right now. I feel like I need to know the results of those lab reports. Both of them."

"Well, I'm sure you're fine on the girly one."

"Oh yeah?"

"Yeah. Those tests are common. You'd know if you talked to anyone about it. Like your mom." Liam scowls across the table.

"I'm not talking to my mom about much these days."

"Do you plan to?" Liam asks.

"I don't know. I'm waiting for the results before I talk to Julie. I don't know about my mom."

"When do you get the results?"

"Wednesday." Jenna and Liam exchange a look. It's the day before Thanksgiving. "I don't know what I'm hoping for. If Bill was my dad, that means my mother has been lying to me my whole life. How do I live with that?"

"Sweetie, you'll figure out a way." Liam takes a sip of his coffee. "Because she has been lying to you your whole life. You're the only one who still thinks it's a question."

"It's not easy for me to believe it." Jenna leans back, folding her arms across herself, gripping her elbows tightly.

"Your mother met Bill nine months before you were born and kept it a secret. Come on. But, if you want to wait 'til Wednesday to deal with it, go ahead." He leans forward and reaches for her hands, prying them loose. "I'll be here whenever you're ready."

Chapter Eleven

On Wednesday, Jenna's on the phone with her doctor, getting the all-clear when the call waiting signal beeps with the lab in Portland calling with their news. It's all quite brief and businesslike and Jenna doesn't feel the way she thinks she should about any of it.

She snaps her cell phone shut. She's sitting on the couch in Sam's apartment. She has a key now, and she hangs out here while he's at work. This way, she can sleep in and lock up herself when she has to go to work.

She likes the quiet here. She likes when the ceiling creaks, likes to imagine what the upstairs neighbor is doing. Sometimes she lets herself in during the afternoon when she knows she'll be alone. She doesn't watch television. She lies on the couch with her legs thrown over the arm, staring vaguely at a rust-colored stain above her head.

She tries that position now, letting it sink in. No cancer. She and Bill Jr. are related. She flips her cell phone open.

"Anticlimactic," she tells Bill Jr. over the phone. She calls to give him the news, but they've already notified him.

"Maybe because you were always my sister," he suggests. "Nothing's really changed."

She knows what he means, and it's sweet, but she can't help the slight irritation she feels at his flippant attitude. *Easy for you to say.*

Everything has changed.

***

Jenna has brunch with Sam at his mother's house. She'll have dinner with her family later in the day. Sam can't leave his mother since his sister is staying in Florida this year, and Jenna can't miss Thanksgiving at her house this year, of all years.

The first Thanksgiving without Bill. The thought has been with her since she woke up this morning, the weight of it. She knows the coming year will be filled with firsts; Christmas and New Year's are a month away. The year ahead will be peppered with these reminders, a minefield. It's exhausting to consider. She hit the snooze button three times.

Cindy sets the table with a basket of croissants and other pastries and an assortment of jams.

"This is my wedding china from my first marriage," she tells Jenna, handing her a stack of three lunch plates. "I used to think it was bad luck to use them but, really, they're just plates." She shrugs. "And I guess if they were lucky, I'd still be married, right?"

"Maybe," Jenna says, smiling. What Jenna is beginning to learn is it could be luckier to get something else besides what you thought you wanted.

The plates are formal and gaudy, a large rosebud in the middle of each plate with smaller ones along the edge. "They don't look like your style," she says as she places them on the table.

"Oh, they're not. You know, I tried to choose what I thought I should want. I remember being worried about what my mother-in-law would think."

Jenna looks at Cindy in her fuchsia kimono and face free of makeup and tries to imagine her as a young woman afraid of what people thought of her.

Sam runs the silverware under the faucet, the water so hot it's making steam. Cindy rambles on, oblivious, and Jenna wonders how this is possible. Of course, days ago she was in the dark herself. Sam is beginning to let her in on his anxieties, things he's only ever talked about with professionals. She never puts her feet up on furniture anymore, and yesterday he paused the movie they were watching to ask her to wash her hands with the antibacterial soap he keeps by the sink. Flushed and unable to look her in the eye, he seemed too vulnerable for her to take offense.

Gripping the silverware, Sam's hands are turning a bright pink under the hot water. Jenna reaches to push the handle, turning it off.

It seems so obvious now she can't believe she missed it. That's how it is with secrets..

***

When Jenna comes in the house, she's surprised by the smell of the turkey cooking. Norman runs to greet her, smells her hands and loses interest when he finds them empty. He resumes his position on the kitchen floor, keeping a close eye on the preparations. Julie stands at the counter, chopping celery.

"Where's Mom?" Jenna asks.

"Sleeping."

Jenna looks at her wrist. It's just after three o'clock.

"She was up earlier." Julie slides the celery chunks off the counter and into her cupped hand. She drops them into a bowl.

"Who put the turkey in?" Jenna shrugs off her coat and hangs it by the door.

"Me."

"What time?" Jenna cracks open the oven door, peering inside.

"An hour ago."

"I said I'd do it."

"I'm not useless."

Jenna looks at her sister, but Julie turns her back and starts slicing an onion.

"Are you okay?" Jenna asks.

"Yep," Julie says brightly, rubbing her eyes with her sleeve.

Jenna looks around the kitchen. There are pots and pans on all the burners. "What can I do?"

"Nothing." Julie's slicing creates a regular thumping sound. It's more precise than you'd imagine for a girl who is unused to cooking.

"Nothing?"

"Sit down and put your feet up. I've got it covered."

Jenna hears something in the false, upbeat tone of her sister's voice. "Julie, come on. What did I do? Are you mad at me?"

"No," she says, but she doesn't turn around.

Jenna reaches for Julie's arm, holding it still. "You have to tell me what's wrong."

Julie looks up, then. "No, I don't." She smiles angrily. "Why don't *you* tell *me*?"

Jenna lets go and Julie resumes her task with the onion, making smaller pieces than necessary.

"Tell you what?"

"Your little secret," Julie says over her shoulder. "The one you think I don't know."

Jenna feels dizzy. She takes a step back and sits at the kitchen table. How could Julie know? Would Bill Jr. have told her? Called to welcome her to the family? Jenna realizes she hadn't specifically asked him not to.

Before she can make sense of this, her mother comes into the room.

"Isn't she something?" Barbara hugs Jenna and motions to her other daughter. "Been at it all day. Who knew she had a domestic side?"

Jenna allows herself to be hugged, but she's relieved when her mother lets her go.

"Well, we're going to have to figure out how to take care of ourselves sooner or later." Julie puts the onion in a skillet. "Jenna won't be around much longer, right Jenna?"

"What's that supposed to mean?" Jenna realizes she hasn't been breathing right since her mother came in.

"You are going back to school in January?" Barbara asks, sitting down.

"Oh." Jenna tries to catch Julie's expression, but her back is still turned. She takes a deep breath. "Yeah, probably."

"Probably?"

"Well, I haven't actually done the paperwork yet."

"Well, you better. No use hanging around here. We have to get back to our lives. That's what Bill would have wanted."

Jenna looks across the table at her mother. She wonders if Bill ever got what he wanted. "You think so?"

"Definitely." Barbara sighs as if this brief interaction has drained her. "It looks like you girls have everything under control." She gets up from the table and wanders back down the hall. Jenna watches her go.

The aroma of cooking onions fills the kitchen. Jenna tries to remember the words she'd planned to use. She hadn't planned to tell Julie today, hadn't wanted to ruin Thanksgiving with this kind of family drama.

"I was going to tell you," she says to Julie's back, the volume of her voice barely above the sizzling skillet.

"You're keeping it?" Julie's face has abandoned anger and is full of genuine concern.

"Keeping what?"

"The baby!"

"Baby?" Jenna feels as if someone has dumped a bucket of icy water over her head. "What baby?"

Julie crosses her arms and narrows her eyes to slits. "I know you're pregnant, Jenna."

Jenna gapes at her sister, wide-eyed. She blinks.

"I ran into Molly at the grocery store yesterday," Julie explains. "Apparently you've already told your coworkers."

Jenna shakes her head, letting out a brief laugh. "Oh, God. That was a joke."

"You told your coworkers you were pregnant as a joke?"

"I didn't say it was a good joke."

Julie eyes her suspiciously. "You're lying."

"I'm not lying!"

"Molly's mother saw you at the OBGYN!"

Jenna closes her eyes, seeing it all through Julie's. "That was something else." She stands up. "I promise. I'm not pregnant."

Julie looks unconvinced. "Then what did you think I was talking about?"

Jenna reaches to turn off all the burners. "Let's go for a drive."

***

They leave a note on the kitchen table in case Barbara wakes up to find them gone. Inside her quiet rage, Jenna struggles for words, and finally manages, *Be back soon.*

They take Norman, mostly because he assumes he's supposed to tag along. Jenna brings his leash but doesn't hook it to his collar. He sits between them with his head up so he can see out the window. At stoplights, he crowds onto Jenna's lap and presses his nose to the glass.

Jenna tells Julie about the Dunkin's smock, the woman with the leaves on her sweater, the way Molly suggested the doctor her mother worked for. By the time they get to the cemetery, they're both laughing.

The parking lot is surprisingly deserted for Thanksgiving. Jenna thought it would be a big visiting holiday.

"It was crowded this morning," Julie mumbles, looking out the window.

Jenna puts the car in park and removes the keys. "You were here?"

"I brought flowers." Julie opens her door and steps outside. Norman jumps down after her.

Jenna hesitates. She thought they might talk in the car, hadn't quite realized where she was going. She hadn't thought this far ahead.

Jenna pulls her coat tight and follows her sister. Norman stops to pee on the first speck of grass, then tramps along at a leisurely pace, distracted by whatever smells he catches on the breeze. Julie heads right for Bill's grave, and Jenna wonders if she would have been able to find it on her own. She hasn't been here since the funeral.

Julie stops on the path suddenly and turns back. "Why were you at the doctor? Molly's mother saw you there."

"I had a bad pap test."

Julie's eyes widen and she brings her hand to her chest.

"I'm fine." Jenna takes Julie's hand and pulls her for the next few steps.

Julie recovers and wraps an arm around Jenna's shoulder, picking up the pace.

There's a bouquet of orange Gerber daisies on Bill's grave. Jenna bends to trace his name on the marble headstone. "How long has this been here?"

"You never come?"

"You do?" Jenna doesn't like cemeteries. She thinks of a song she heard in her childhood:

The worms crawl in, the worms crawl out,

The worms play pinochle on your snout!

Julie sits cross-legged in the grass. "Yeah. I come here to think."

Jenna considers her pants and then sits down anyway. "What do you think about?"

"Oh, you know, what I should be doing with my life. What he'd tell me to do."

"Would he? Tell you what to do?" Jenna can't remember Bill giving much advice.

"Yeah. 'Be more like Jenna.'" Julie smiles.

"No." Jenna bumps her shoulder against Julie's. "He loved you just the way you are."

Julie sighs. "Yeah. I guess you're right." She rearranges the bouquet against the headstone.

They sit together in the chilly quiet. Norman finds them, then lays on top of Bill's grave with his head between his paws. He looks like he's pouting. It's eerie, as if he knows where he is. Jenna thinks she believes in God and heaven because she likes the idea; she doesn't believe in ghosts or the devil because she doesn't. She's fairly sure this is flimsy logic.

"So, is it about Bill?" Julie asks.

"What?"

"What you have to tell me."

"Yeah." Jenna pulls a clump of brown grass out of the ground. It leaves a naked spot like a wound in the earth. "He told me something while he was sick, I didn't really believe at first. I thought he was confused. But turns out it was true."

"What?"

"Bill and mom met each other before we were born. They had a—" Jenna struggles to say the word aloud. "An affair."

"Before we were born?"

Jenna nods. "Less than nine months before."

Julie's eyes widen and the color leaves her face. Her upper body sways, and she sets a hand on Bill's headstone to steady herself.

"Are you okay?"

"I didn't eat breakfast," she says, closing her eyes.

"Put your head between your knees," Jenna says, and Julie obeys. She wraps her arms around her knees and lets her head fall forward.

Julie has a long history of passing out from missing breakfast. Getting ready for school in the morning, she often spent too much time in the shower or, more likely, hit snooze on her alarm clock too many times. She'd fly out of the house without eating and be in the nurse's office by homeroom. Jenna started cooking a bunch of hard-boiled eggs at the beginning of the week and would keep them in the fridge so she could hand one to Julie on her way out the door.

"This is crazy," Julie says.

"I didn't think it was true at first, either."

"No, *this*." Julie sweeps an arm around herself to indicate the two of them huddled on Bill's grave, Julie holding her head between her knees while Jenna crouches over her. "We must look ridiculous."

Jenna takes stock of the cemetery. Norman picks up his head for a moment, looking at them. He sets it back down. "There's no one here." She rubs Julie's back. "Take some deep breaths."

After a few moments, Julie sits up again. "What made you change your mind? How do you know it's true?"

"I had a DNA test."

"A DNA test?"

"With Bill Jr."

"Bill Jr?" she says, dismissively, as if she is saying, *the milkman*. "Why didn't you tell me?"

"I don't know. I didn't want to upset you and be wrong. He told me the night before he died and then everything got busy with the funeral and everything."

"And Mom?"

"I haven't said anything to her. When he told me, he made me promise I wouldn't tell her, like he was afraid he'd get in trouble. I couldn't ask her without proof. I mean, she's lied to us all these years."

Julie stands and brushes off her pants. She walks a few steps and leans against a tree with her back to Jenna.

"We can talk to Mom together," Jenna says.

Julie turns to her with tears in her eyes, still leaning on the tree. "We can't."

"What do you mean?"

"You said. Bill made you promise not to tell her. This was his dying wish."

Jenna isn't sure she agrees, but she isn't going to do anything without Julie's agreement. They're in this together now. It belongs to each of them equally.

"Are you going to be okay getting through the rest of the day without talking about what's going on in your head?" Jenna asks.

Julie shrugs. "Why not? We do it all the time." She extends an arm to Jenna, who takes her hand and pulls herself to her feet. "But now that I know you're not pregnant, you better help with the cooking."

***

When Jenna tells Sam Julie thought she was pregnant, he laughs with the confidence of a man who is not having sex with his girlfriend.

Jenna didn't mean to wait this long. Sam is a beautiful distraction from the mess of her life. He is patient, letting her set the pace whenever things get physical. She isn't sure what she's waiting for or how to know when they get there. She wants to feel like she can give him her full attention.

That night in his bed, they spoon in their underwear.

"So, you guys were like 'Pass the cranberry sauce' all day?" Sam asks. He seems to be having a hard time picturing her Thanksgiving dinner.

"Pretty much." Jenna locks her fingers in his. "It didn't last very long. After we cooked so much food, she barely ate anything. She had a few bites, wandered into the den, and fell asleep in Bill's chair. I covered her with a blanket before I left."

"Must be hard to be mad at someone who needs to be tucked in."

Jenna doesn't want to remember the way her mother looked sleeping, her drooping face and her slightly open mouth. "I made green bean casserole, and nobody touched it. Turns out, Bill was the one who liked it."

"I like green bean casserole," Sam says, kissing her shoulder.

"Well, lucky you, I brought you leftovers."

"I'm sorry." Sam squeezes her tighter and they lie quietly for several minutes. "Do you think—" His voice trails off.

Jenna looks at him over her shoulder. "What?"

She sees the struggle on his face as he weighs his words carefully. "Do you feel powerful keeping something from her for a change? The tables have turned?"

Jenna rolls the idea around in her head like butterscotch candy. "I don't think that's it," she says after a moment. "Julie says we can never tell because it was Bill's dying wish."

"Do you believe that?"

Jenna sighs. "Not really. Bill would want us to do what was best for us, but I'm not sure what that is."

"Can you have a relationship with your mother with this secret between you?"

"I think I'm more afraid we won't be able to have one when this comes out."

"What do you mean?"

"My mother and grandmother haven't spoken to each other for most of my life. I never understood how that could happen. But now, I do." Jenna pulls Sam's arms tighter around her body. "And it terrifies me. I'm afraid of this anger inside me, of what will happen if I let it out. I think that's the thing I fear the most." She shivers. "I've already lost my father."

"They say it's good to say your fears out loud."

"They?"

Sam holds her for several minutes, as the tension drains slowly from her body. "I love this curve," he says, his finger tracing the slope from her hip to her waist and back again.

Jenna smiles into her pillow as he kisses the back of her neck. The day's clothing lay crumpled on the floor: Sam's dress socks and khakis, her socks with the turkeys on them, and a pale blue, button-up blouse. She likes wearing shirts with buttons. When she dresses in the morning, she imagines how Sam will unbutton them, slowly, like he's unwrapping his last Christmas present.

"Is it driving you crazy we haven't had sex yet?" Jenna asks, surprising herself with her bluntness. It helps that Sam can't see her face.

He gives her a squeeze. "Not at all," he says.

Sometimes, Jenna thinks, lying is the kindest thing to do.

"I am comforted you used the word *yet*," he admits.

And they laugh.

***

Jenna wakes before the morning has given up the darkness. She slips from the bed and gathers her clothes, dressing quietly in the bathroom. She stands in the doorway to watch Sam sleep, his eyes moving rapidly beneath his eyelids, and she wishes she knew what he was dreaming about. The note she leaves him is both inadequate and unnecessary. *I love you*, it says.

There's a different kind of note waiting for her when she gets home. Her mother's car is missing from the driveway, making Jenna's early morning return a wasted gesture. The lined yellow paper is folded in thirds; in blue ink, her mother has written:

Girls.

Jenna sits at the table and unfolds the page without turning on the kitchen lights.

I'm doing this all wrong, I know. And I'm sorry. I can't be in the house right now. Bill is everywhere.

There's more. She's going to stay with a friend in Boston for a few days. Jenna struggles to think of which of her mother's friends live in Boston. Then she's off to San Diego for work. *Keeping busy,* Barbara writes, *is the only thing that helps.*

Bill *is* everywhere. The blue chair. The painting that hung in the living room, taking up the entire wall. Some unidentified mountain range he loved even though it didn't go with anything else in the room. He renovated the kitchen after his retirement when he needed a project. He'd picked out and installed everything himself. He was so proud of the kitchen.

The letter isn't much, but it may be the first time Jenna's mother has made any attempt to explain herself to her daughters. Barbara had slept through the holiday and then packed a suitcase, put on her face, and left the house while it was still dark. Jenna imagines her tiptoeing down the front steps and wonders whether she'd noticed the car that wasn't there.

Jenna doesn't blame her mother for her coping technique. She might be on to something. It's hard to grieve properly when you feel responsible for other grieving people. Maybe they should all get away from each other. But then, who would take care of Julie? And Norman.

At this thought, Jenna feels panic creeping up her spine. Where's Norman? Why hadn't he run to the door when she came in? She opens the basement door and whispers his name into the darkness. When he doesn't appear, she calls out louder. Nothing.

She shrugs her winter coat off onto the living room floor and runs upstairs. Her bedroom is empty, the bed unmade and the moon still visible out the window. Julie's door is closed. She turns the knob slowly and pushes in.

Norman is curled like a fuzzy caterpillar at the foot of Julie's bed. He lifts his head as Jenna enters the room. She sighs, shaking her head and laughing at herself. She has become too used to predicting disasters.

Julie stirs as Jenna sits on the edge of the bed, rubbing her face into Norman's soft fur. "Jen?" she murmurs with her eyes closed.

"Move over," Jenna says, and Julie makes room for her to lay down. Norman crawls between them.

"You okay?" Julie mumbles into her pillow.

"Yeah." Jenna kicks off her shoes and gets under the blanket. "Go back to sleep." Jenna scratches Norman's head. She doesn't blame her mother for leaving. She blames her for other things maybe, but not that.

Before Bill got sick, they were the kind of parents who embarrassed their children. They kissed each other with open mouths, unlike the sexless pecks Jenna had witnessed between the mothers and fathers of her friends. Bill used to ogle Barbara appreciatively when she wore a low-cut blouse or her bathing suit. He'd pat her rear end when she walked by. They made each other giggle. Often. All the time.

She knows her mother loved Bill, and the pain she's having seems to trump anything else. Jenna has her own version of that pain, and it obliterates the rest of her feelings, even the anger. The pain is what she feels most; sometimes it's all there is, all that matters.

Norman kicks her with his back legs, and her eyes fly open. She scowls at him, but he's asleep, running in his dreams. Jenna closes her eyes again, vaguely wondering what he's dreaming about.

Chapter Twelve

On the first of December, Julie insists they get a Christmas tree. When Jenna indicates she already has plans with Sam that evening, Julie suggests he joins them. They drive to a little tree farm in Bedford and weave between the tall evergreens, regarding them like mannequins, judging their wares. *This one has a bare spot; this one is too short.* They choose one that's about six feet tall and decide the bare spot can be turned to the wall. A man in a striped ski hat and fingerless gloves takes Jenna's fifty dollars and helps Sam tie it to the roof of the Camry with blue twine.

It takes all three of them to maneuver the tree up the steps into the house. They talk to each other in the clipped, sharp tones of frustration inevitable with a project like this. By the time they're huffing and puffing, holding it upright in the living room while Julie runs to the basement to get the tree stand, Jenna and Sam have already had enough.

"You said left."

"I meant *my* left."

Julie returns to the basement while they anchor the tree, bringing up the three boxes of decorations. She puts water in the tree stand and leaves them to untie the mass of lights.

It's never the thing Jenna thinks will trigger Sam's compulsion that actually does. He digs through the musty cardboard box, pulling out cords without stopping to consider what kind of bugs might be inside. He never balks at patting Norman who drools and is dirty the way dogs are always dirty, although he goes to the groomer regularly.

She knows when he gets home, he'll take his shoes off in the kitchen and step from the linoleum to the carpet in his socks.

And he will wash his hands with the antibacterial soap. If he needs to go back into the kitchen, he'll put his shoes on again and there will be more hand washing. It appears to be important the bottoms of his shoes have no contact with the carpeting, the furniture. Jenna's trying to figure out the rules, but she's finding it may be less about logic and more about ritual.

They sit next to each other with a pile of cords on their laps.

"Did you leave cookies for Santa when you were little?" Sam asks.

"Not really." This used to be Bill's job. He always took the most practical task while Barbara chose Christmas carols and helped the girls with the fun decorations. Last year, Jenna sat on the couch and assisted, doing most of the untangling herself and hoping he didn't notice. "Did you?"

"No," Sam says. "But I thought everyone else did. I remember when I realized the rest of my class left him cookies. I felt bad."

"Were you worried your presents wouldn't be as good?"

Sam elbows her in the ribs. "I don't think it was that."

She elbows him back. "If you say so."

They're quiet for some minutes, concentrating.

"Maybe it has to do with whether your parents have a sweet tooth," Sam suggests.

"Maybe. I don't know. Bill liked cookies."

Once Jenna had uncovered the mystery of Santa, she always associated him with Bill, not her mother. She imagined him staying up late, filling stockings and putting together bicycles and dollhouses.

Bill was always the *parent*. He was the one who looked over report cards and detentions and permission slips. He was the one to call when Jenna found herself stranded without a ride home. He was the one she went to when petitioning for a later curfew or the right to get her ears pierced. Of course, it was

Barbara who brought the girls to the mall on their tenth birthday, stood over the glass case pointing out tiny gold studs, squealing. But Bill put his foot down when they begged at seven, eight, and nine. It was Bill who relented, allowed, decided.

Sam pulls a strand of lights free and reaches to plug it into the wall. "Did you call your advisor?" he asks.

"Not yet." Some of the lights flash on and some don't.

"What are you waiting for?"

Jenna tightens a bulb, lighting an entire section. She glares at him without answering.

"When does the semester start?"

"Not 'til January."

"That's soon."

Jenna sighs. "You know, I'll be two hours away."

"So?"

Jenna can't tell if he's not concerned about long distance relationships or if he's not planning to have one. She waits for him to say more.

Instead, she hears the front door bang. Her mother appears in the doorway.

"You're home," Jenna says, stating the obvious.

"You got a tree," Barbara reciprocates, staring at the evergreen like an unexpected, unwelcome house guest.

"Yeah. Do you like it?" Jenna looks at the tree, which suddenly looks crooked.

Barbara sighs. "I thought we might skip it this year."

"The tree or the holiday?" Jenna asks.

"Both."

Jenna's face falls.

"I could take the tree to my place," Sam offers.

"Oh, it's fine." Barbara forces a smile. "I'm being silly. It's a lovely tree, Jenna." Barbara unbuttons her coat. "I probably won't be here for Christmas anyway."

"What?" Jenna gets up from the couch and follows her mother into the kitchen where she's hanging her coat. Sam stays put. "You have to work over Christmas?"

"No, no." Barbara rummages through her handbag. "I'm looking at taking a cruise." She fans out the stack of brochures on the kitchen table. "See? I'm leaning toward ten days, but possibly more like two weeks."

Jenna listens closely while her mother talks about snorkeling and pina coladas but doesn't hear an invitation.

"You're going away by yourself for Christmas?"

"Well, not exactly. I'd go with a friend. That's what we talked about while I was in Boston."

Jenna sits at the table, leafing through glossy pictures of Puerto Vallarta, Hawai'i, and the Florida Keys. She can see the appeal of escaping the forced merriment of Christmas, the excruciating nostalgia. "Who's your friend in Boston? I can't remember."

"Doug Whitman." Barbara continues to search her handbag.

Jenna's head jerks to attention. "Doug? Who's he?"

"You remember Doug. He came to dinner that time. We used to work together."

"No," Jenna says, flatly. She does not remember this man. All her mother's friends have names like Judy, Pam, and Carol. She's quite sure she would remember a Doug.

Barbara shrugs. "I must have a nail file in the bathroom," she says, absently, and she leaves the room.

Sam comes into the kitchen a minute later and finds Jenna sitting at the table, holding tightly to a brochure of the Caribbean.

***

"So, my mom has a boyfriend," she tells Liam the next night over Fajitas and mudslides. The restaurant is busy, and there are lots of noisy people.

"You're kidding."

Jenna shrugs. "Maybe they're friends. *We're* friends." She motions between the two of them.

"Is he gay?"

"He sent her flowers. *For a wonderful weekend.* They came this morning."

"He's not gay."

Jenna finishes her drink. The interior walls are painted every color imaginable. The one behind Liam is turquoise with yellow streaked across, becoming a yellow wall splattered with hot pink. Under a layer of glass, their table is lime green.

"Where did they meet?"

"They used to work together. That's all I know."

There are masks with animal faces hanging from the walls—a zebra, a toucan. Even the hollows of their eyes appear to be aimed at Jenna.

"You didn't grill her about it?" Liam asks.

"I was too stunned."

"Let's get you another drink."

Jenna tilts her glass, looking inside and finding it empty. "I think I'm already tipsy."

"I'm driving." He catches the waiter's eye. This time, she gets a strawberry daiquiri.

"They're going on a cruise together. A cruise! How tacky is that?"

Bill would never have gone on a cruise. He didn't like crowds or boats. Or elevators.

Liam shakes his head. "Has your mother ever been single?"

Jenna looks up at the ceiling. The multi-colored glass chandeliers spin and sway in a breeze she doesn't feel on her skin. "In the revised version of her life," she says, looking back at Liam, "you know, the *true* one, I'd have to say no."

He liked the beach, though. Last summer, they spent an afternoon at Rye Beach. He sat under an umbrella, watching other people frolic in the freezing waves. But before they left, he told them he wanted to get his feet wet. Jenna rolled up his pant legs, but they ended up getting wet anyway. She should have done one more roll.

Liam jumps, startling himself with his own thought. "Do you think they were together before Bill died?"

Jenna moans. "I can't think about it."

"Sorry." He pauses, thoughtfully. "Maybe it isn't too bad. I mean, your mother must have been lonely the last couple of years. She didn't really have a partner."

Jenna glares at him across the table.

"But you're not thinking about it. So, I'll shut up."

"Thanks." One more roll would have been enough to keep the cuffs dry; as it was, the salt water soaked through each folded layer, making the entire effort pointless. She may as well not have bothered at all.

Jenna's drink comes and she has a little too much trouble getting her lips to meet the straw. Once she does, she doesn't let go. She sucks in fast and then sits back in her seat, holding the bridge of her nose.

"Brain freeze?"

She nods and Liam giggles. "I have news," he says in a sing song. "The landlord from our old building has a unit available in January."

"Doesn't he think we're screw-ups for leaving in the middle of a semester?"

"He didn't seem to. I mean, come on, who can stay mad at us?"

Jenna laughs at this and at Liam's silly, blurry face.

"He said we could come look at it next week."

Jenna continues to laugh, but she's not sure why.

"Okay?"

"Okay!" She yells and pounds her fist on the table. Liam shushes her, so she shushes him right back.

***

Jenna decides it makes more sense to have Liam drop her at Sam's. She calls from the car, and he meets her at the front door in his flannel pants and T-shirt. He waves to Liam, locks up and finds Jenna's drunkenness amusing for about five minutes.

She sits on the bed and plays with his hair while he helps her with her sneakers. He tries to get her under the covers while she tries to pull his shirt off.

"Jenna, come on. I have to get up for work in about four hours."

"Work, shmerk," she mumbles, pulling him on top of her and kissing him. He kisses her back for a while, but when her hands begin to slip beneath the waistband of his pajamas, he pulls away.

"What's a matter?" Jenna flutters her eyelashes at him, and he can't help laughing.

"Baby, I'm tired." He runs his hands through her hair. "And you're *drunk*."

Jenna scoffs as if offended. "Not really."

"Oh, no?"

"Maybe a little." She holds her thumb and index finger half an inch apart.

Sam nods, sitting up and trying to arrange the blankets. "Let's go to sleep."

"No," she whines, pulling at his shirt again, kissing the back of his neck. "Let's just do it. Let's get it over with."

He shakes her off. "Jesus, Jenna!" He looks over his shoulder at her. "That's real sexy. That's what every guy wants to hear."

Drunk as she is, tears spring to her eyes. Sam shakes his head. "This is not a fight," he says slowly, like he's speaking to a child. "You get a pass this time 'cause your drunk. But don't push it. Go to sleep."

She falls back and turns away from him. He pulls the blanket over her and kisses her cheek. In the morning, Sam slams kitchen cabinets he didn't really need to open while Jenna buries her head and groans. He sings in the shower, playing drums on the shampoo bottles. He gets dressed with the lights on and sits on Jenna's side of the bed as he rifles through his sock drawer and then walks around the room in search of his wallet, which is in his back pocket the whole time.

"Hey, Jenna."

"Mmm?"

He sits next to her and pulls the pillow off her head. "I changed my mind."

Jenna winces in the light. "About what?"

"Let's just do it," Sam says, tugging the blanket. "Let's get it over with."

Jenna rolls away. "I'm sorry!" Her voice is muffled by the mattress. "I'm an idiot."

"Yeah, you are." Sam laughs, throwing the blanket over her again.

***

The plan was for Jenna and Julie to take their mom to The Back Room for her birthday, but Barbara expands on this idea, and the girls can't find the words to argue. It's her day. Why shouldn't she bring a friend if she wants?

This is how Jenna finds herself sitting across from Doug in a dimly lit restaurant. The five of them are sitting in a u-shaped booth: Jenna, Sam, Julie, Barbara, Doug. They took separate cars and met for the first time in front of the host's podium. Jenna had offered her hand, but he pulled her into a hug.

He must be in his late fifties but manages to look like a gawky teenager with gray hair. The truth is he could be lovely, and Jenna would still hate him. Lucky for her, he isn't lovely. He's loud and boring. He tells a joke about sweet and sour soup causing Chinese people to have slanty eyes. And then he laughs and laughs.

Jenna grips the edges of her menu. Sam rubs her back and leans closer. "Breathe," he suggests.

"Have you ever been up the Kancamagus Highway?" It's the only question he asks all night, but he doesn't wait for an answer. "It's a fantastic way to see the foliage in the fall. I took your mother up this year. We had a wonderful time."

"We sure did," Barbara says, nodding and grinning. "And we're going hiking as soon as it gets warm enough, right?"

"Since when do you *hike*?" Jenna doesn't hide the contempt in her voice.

Barbara shrugs.

"Yeah, we're gonna go to the White Mountains," Doug says, nodding. "First, we'll go to the flume. It used to be a gorge with a huge boulder wedged across the top, hanging down." Doug positions his hands in a way that's meant to represent this. At least, that's how it appears to Jenna. Not having any idea what a flume or a gorge is, the hand signals don't clarify. "But a hundred years ago it was knocked down in a storm. It's still an interesting gorge, though." He nods some more, in apparent agreement with himself. "It's near where the old man in the mountain used to be. We could see that, too. Not that there's anything left to see." Doug doesn't slow down until the food comes.

"It's a short hike," Barbara says, taking a bite of her salad.

"Yeah, about a mile, I think." Doug picks up the steak knife with the big wooden handle. When they came here with Bill, he always joked Barbara should sneak them into her purse. He'd never seen knives so formidable.

"Oh, a mile. Sounds great." Jenna doesn't think it sounds great at all. But she thinks about the hard time she and Julie gave Bill at the beginning, and it takes all the fun out of anything else she could say.

They used to come to The Back Room for all kinds of family celebrations. Bill always ordered the prime rib, bloody. At every restaurant he frequented, Bill had one favorite meal: the fried clam dinner at Newick's. Short ribs at Friday's. At Ruby's Diner, it was shepherd's pie.

There's not much conversation while they all shovel food in their mouths. At one point, Doug interrupts the silence to say he's only seen a moose once. "Right alongside the highway probably less than half a mile from my house."

Jenna can't think of anything to say to this. She looks at Julie, who's focused on her plate. Barbara is nodding with her mouth full and smiling like an idiot. Sam offers his own moose story, something about finding one standing in the road, waiting several minutes for the animal to move along and knowing better than to honk his horn.

"Maybe he was nervous," Sam says once Barbara and Doug leave.

"Maybe." They didn't stay for dessert to make it to the movie.

When the check arrives, Julie puts in a twenty.

"Where did this come from?" Jenna asks, smoothing it against the table.

"Rainy day pile."

"Is it raining?"

"Seems like it."

Jenna sighs, closing the cash into the leather folder. She looks past Sam to her sister. "So, you realize they drove the Kancamagus in the fall?" She doesn't say the rest: Bill died in the fall, and his birthday was in the fall. Her mother had spent one of Bill's last days remarking on the beautiful foliage with this ridiculous man.

Julie puts her elbows on the table and covers her face. "Can't we pretend this isn't happening?"

"For how long?"

Julie slides her hands from her eyes to her forehead, looking at Jenna through tears. "Forever?"

Jenna's impulse is to do whatever she can to keep Julie from crying. She takes a deep breath and holds it, waiting for this impulse to pass.

***

The next morning, there's a thin layer of snow on Jenna's windowsill. She closes the window and locks it, looking out into the yard. It must be several feet deep out there. She can hear the groan of the snowplow coming up the road. For now, the street hasn't been touched; its pristine white blends seamlessly with the smooth expanse of snowy lawn. The only indication of the boundaries underneath is the stubby mailbox, its red flag pointing upward, oblivious and hopeful.

Jenna goes into the bathroom to pee. The house is still quiet; it's much too early for Julie to be awake. Barbara is probably reading in bed, some trashy romance novel or murder mystery she picked up at an airport. Jenna hates airports, can't imagine having to spend so much of her life there. She's always hated them, but the added hassles at security have made them worse.

These days, after passing through the metal detectors and x-ray machines, she starts feeling trapped and claustrophobic, forced to spend three dollars for a water, listen to the garbled intercom for her boarding group, and spend several hours sandwiched into an itty-bitty chair, breathing recycled air.

Spending so much time away, Barbara must have a different sense of what home means. Jenna isn't exactly sure whether it would mean more or less, but she has formed certain theories over the years.

At the top of the stairs, Jenna's surprised she doesn't smell coffee. When Barbara's home, she usually requires it. It's one of the few domestic chores she can be expected to perform. Jenna has long associated the smell of coffee with her mother's presence—a reassuring sign the family is together, complete.

It can't really mean that anymore and yet. And yet.

Although it's tempting to slip back into the warmth of her bed, Jenna starts down the stairs. She isn't a regular coffee drinker, but she certainly knows how to make it. She finds the paper filters in a drawer and adds a rounded scoop of coffee grounds. She considers again the endless mystery of why coffee never tastes as good as it smells.

Jenna fills the coffee pot at the sink, looking out the window. She hadn't been expecting snow; she never listens to the weather. Bill listened to it fanatically in his last years, even on days he had no plans to leave the house. The white has lost its purity. The plow has been by, carving a path through the snow, a deep gouge already dirty with salt and sand and tire tracks. Jenna notices something she'd missed when she looked out the window upstairs. Her mother's car is not in the driveway.

As the water begins to flow over the lip of the coffee pot, Jenna reaches to turn off the faucet.

Without wanting to, she pictures her mother wrapped in motel sheets, giggling with Doug. Perhaps the storm caught her by surprise, ruining her plans to be home before her daughters woke up.

Jenna's stomach churns. She lifts the pot and pours the water down the drain. It occurs to her that she should be worried. Barbara's car could be off in a ditch while she sits quite innocently in an emergency room. Or lies in a coma.

Reaching to turn the water on again, Jenna fills the pot carefully, just to the red line. She longs for that reassuring smell even if it represents a lie she's choosing to tell herself one last time.

As often as she tries to give people the benefit of the doubt, they're never really in comas when they should be.

***

Hours later, when Jenna leaves for work, Barbara still hasn't returned. Julie sleeps in, as usual, leaving Jenna alone with her quiet rage. On her way out the door, she pours out the contents of the coffee pot without pouring herself a cup. She doesn't like to think of her mother coming through the door and feeling a warm welcome. If she wants coffee, she can make some herself.

The holiday donuts are covered in green icing with red and white sprinkles. The green is too bright and unnatural to consider eating, though obviously people do. Jenna doesn't imagine it would taste sweet; she imagines the waxy flavor of a melted crayon. It makes her gag. She looks away.

"Morning sickness?" Ashley asks, tipping her head in a presentation of concern.

Jenna sighs. "I'm not pregnant."

Ashley stands up straighter, her eyes wide. She wears too much mascara, and her lashes are prickly darks tufts, the entwined legs of a dead, dehydrated tarantula. "What happened?"

"I was never pregnant," Jenna says, feeling like she has emerged from the ocean, like she's been fighting against the tide only to realize how easy it is to let the waves carry her to the shore.

She's had the power all along.

"You lied?" Ashley doesn't appear offended. Just curious.

"I didn't have to." Jenna gestures to her uniform. "Someone made an assumption, and I never corrected them. It seemed easier."

"Oh." Ashley nods, but her face remains scrunched. "Huh."

"It snowballed," Jenna says, and she remembers how Liam used this term to explain her mother's deception, to describe the way the truth can slip through your fingers, escaping your control. She wonders if honesty might not be the simple thing she's grown up believing in. Sometimes the truth is a decision that needs to be guarded at every moment, chosen again and again and again.

Chapter Thirteen

The landlord reminds Jenna of a character from *The Muppet Show*, the round blue man who is frustrated by Grover's poor wait service. Mr. Lewis isn't blue, but he is mustached with bushy patches of hair on each side of his head, bald straight down the middle. He hurries around the room, opening the shades. This is a different unit from the one she and Liam shared last fall. It's on the third floor, at the backside of the building, away from the traffic of the street below.

Mr. Lewis opens the door to the small balcony. "In the summer, the sun shines on this side."

The summer, Jenna thinks. Now, she folds her arms against the wintery gust, and Mr. Lewis takes the hint and pulls the door closed.

Liam looks in the bathroom and turns to her. "About the same. What do you think?"

"It's another flight of stairs," Jenna mumbles.

"The ceilings are higher," Mr. Lewis counters.

Liam lifts his eyebrows and smiles in agreement.

Jenna frowns. "I never hit my head on the other ones."

`Liam turns to Mr. Lewis. "Could we have a few minutes to talk it over?"

"Take your time," the man says, hitching up his pants. He walks to the door, his footsteps loud on the floorboards, echoing in the empty room.

When he's gone, Liam hoists himself onto the kitchen counter. "What's your deal?"

"What?"

"You're being moody."

"Moody?" Jenna smiles. "Is that a euphemism?"

Liam tries to arrange his face into something resembling innocence, but he can't stop himself from laughing. "Are we gonna do this or what?"

Jenna sighs. She can't exactly explain what her hesitancy is about. It feels strange to be making decisions about the future. "It's hard, you know. This moving on business." She tries to sound flippant, but her throat feels constricted.

Liam hops off the counter and walks toward her with his arms open. "I know. But the alternative is living with your mother." He holds her by her forearms and looks into her eyes. "I can't be worse than that. I'm taking my meds, I promise."

"Well, when you put it like that."

Barbara is rarely home these days. She's vague about her whereabouts and Jenna chooses to feign ignorance. Julie refuses to talk about any of it. It's unhealthy, Jenna knows, but somehow it feels safer to leave everything unacknowledged.

Liam walks to the center of the room. "The higher ceilings really do make it look bigger."

Jenna has heard of women who pretend not to know their husbands are cheating. Knowing they've been betrayed isn't what makes the relationship disintegrate; it's the forced confrontation. Once everything is in the open, they must stand up for themselves.

It feels like that. A betrayal too big to be forgiven is better ignored.

"Did you know twins can have different fathers?" Liam asks, fingering the Venetian blinds.

"Oh, God."

"It's a real thing. I googled it."

Jenna walks to the other window, peeking out the slats at the patch of pale grass surrounded by a chain link fence and piles of dirty snow. "I know, but shit." Jenna pushes her bangs out of her eyes. "As if things aren't screwed up enough."

"It might explain a few things."

"Oh, really?"

"Yeah. Like why you and Julie don't look alike."

"We're *fraternal*."

"Or—" Liam holds up a finger. "You're *half*-sisters."

Jenna shakes her head. "You watch too many soap operas."

"I gave them up." Liam stands on his tiptoes and reaches for the ceiling. His fingertips don't graze the surface.

"Impressive," Jenna says, humoring him.

"Right?"

Mr. Lewis taps at the door and pushes it open. "So, what's the verdict?"

Jenna puts her hand on Liam's arm, reigning in his enthusiasm. "Can we paint the walls?" she asks.

"I don't see why not."

"We'll take it," Jenna says, and Liam starts clapping and jumping around.

***

She googles it too, of course. Bi-paternal twins. Also called heteropaternal superfecundation. She saw a show about it once, years ago, but she hadn't paid much attention. It's more common than she would have thought. Only two percent of the world's population is made up of fraternal twins. Of those, one set out of every twelve is bi-paternal.

Jenna grabs a pen and scribbles some general numbers on a Post-it note. By her math, there are millions of bi-paternal twins in the world. The relative newness of DNA testing and the obvious social taboo has kept the phenomenon hush-hush.

Wikipedia claims it's more common in prostitutes and animals. Most litters of puppies have multiple fathers.

Jenna scratches out the numbers, writing lines in one direction and then the other. She rips the paper into tiny shreds and flushes them down the toilet.

***

Jenna puts in her last day at Dunkin' Donuts a week before Christmas. She works the late shift, and before closing for the night, she rescues all the honey glazed from the morning dumpsters.

And one Boston Kreme.

The snow has melted. Today it rained. Jenna chooses her footsteps carefully, her boots sinking here and there, the mud coloring the edges of her heel a reddish brown.

She doesn't get lost, as she thought she might. She ends up right where she intended, standing in front of the still not-quite-familiar headstone, reading the name carved into the granite.

"Bill." She sighs. She doesn't like to imagine his body rotting in the earth beneath her, already food for the worms and bugs. She wishes they'd had him cremated. That seems better somehow, more civilized. They could have scattered his ashes into the river, into the wind, and let him be gone. She doesn't like to think of his body existing in a place. She knows he isn't there, isn't anywhere.

And yet here she is, talking to a big gray rock with his name on it. Here she is, reaching into a white paper bag, pulling out his favorite donut and placing it on the headstone's cold, smooth arch.

She pulls her coat closer around her body. "I don't know what to do," she says. "Any ideas?"

There's no voice in the breeze. She reaches back into the bag and bites into the sugary glazed donut, so sweet it makes her jaw ache. She needs to sit Julie down, force her to talk. They have to go to their mother together. Keeping secrets like this isn't good for anyone. The crumbs scatter at her feet. They'll be gobbled up by rodents or birds along with her Egyptian offering to Bill.

Jenna doesn't wait to see it, though. She walks back to the car, shaking her head at the impulse that brought her here. She takes the highway, driving past her own exit to the west side of town. The bad part. The buildings are more run down here, the sides often *tagged* with undecipherable spray paint. And yet, she never feels unsafe.

If Bill dying is a door closing in Jenna's life, Sam is the open window.

She turns her key in the lock and walks into the dark kitchen. She sets the donut bag on the counter and hangs her coat over a kitchen chair. Light spills down the hallway from the bedroom. Jenna kicks off her boots and crosses over to the carpet in her socks. There are clumps of dried mud left on the linoleum and she makes a mental note to clean it up before Sam sees it.

But first, she tiptoes down the hall.

"I brought home sugar-coated carbs," she says, leaning her hip against the door frame.

Sam lowers his book. *Ishmael.* "I already brushed."

Jenna shrugs. "Breakfast, then." She sits on the edge of the bed and kisses him. He drops the book, his hands going to her hair, losing his place.

They still haven't had sex, but they've had a lot of time to get to know each other's bodies. The first time he went down on her, she tried to stop him, imagining the awkwardness of her failure to climax, or the more awkward fake orgasm she'd have to enact. But even as she arranged the words in her mind, they evaporated. There was a loosening low and deep in her abdomen. She arched her back and closed her eyes, for the first time allowing herself to make the noises she'd always tried to hold in. Afterward, his kiss tasted like her, and all she'd been able to manage to say to him, breathlessly, was "How?"

She still feels that way about him. How does he know the right way to touch her? How does he know what she's thinking?

Amazingly, Jenna's finding it does work both ways. She notices the days he washes his hands less, and she knows how he beats himself up on the days he must wash them more. He stopped asking her to join in. His therapist told him he was turning her into an enabler. Sometimes, she forgets and puts her feet on the couch, but it's okay. It's something they're working on.

Jenna goes into the bathroom to pee and brush her teeth. She ties her hair back with an elastic she wears around her wrist. Her bangs escape its reach, and she scowls at her reflection.

When she climbs into bed next to him, Sam places the book in his lap. "How was your last day?"

Jenna tilts her head, trying to think of the right one-word summary. "Over?"

Sam nods. "Over, it is."

"Where are you?" Jenna asks, motioning to the book. She read it first. She recommended it.

"Ishmael explained when you give food to starving people, they have babies, and then you have more starving people."

"Right."

"I don't know what to do with that."

"I know."

When they cook together, he's her sous chef. He chops the veggies for the stir fry, cuts the slimy chicken breast into bites. These are the parts of cooking she finds tedious. Now she throws it together in the skillet, experiments with spices and marinades. They're a team and they make a good one.

"I stopped by the cemetery," Jenna says.

"How was that?"

"Weird."

He waits for her to say more, but she doesn't. "Want to lay on me?"

"Yeah." Jenna snuggles closer and puts her head on his chest.

***

Before she leaves, Barbara places their gifts under the tree. Each stack of boxes is wrapped in identical paper—silver snowflakes on a light blue background. They're professionally wrapped, clearly all from the same store. Jenna imagines the hour or so she spent at Macy's or Target or some other department store, filling her cart with objects that would get her off the hook, would allow her to escape.

This is only confirmed on Christmas morning when Jenna and Julie sit cross legged on the floor in the living room and unwrap them: Cashmere sweaters, perfume, jewelry boxes, scarves, and gloves.

"At least they're different colors," Jenna says, holding the teal sweater to her chest.

Julie presses the tissue paper and closes hers back into the box. "It doesn't really feel like Christmas."

Jenna sighs. She should have put on the old cassette tape of Christmas carols. Her favorites were the classics: Bing Crosby, Nat King Cole, Johnny Mathis. Bill always joined in for the oldies, the ones he knew. She can still hear his deep voice singing, "Chestnuts roasting on an open fire." Those days were the only time he ever sang. Every year it surprised her all over again he could carry a tune.

Jenna has no interest in covers sung by contemporary artists. The closest exception she makes is John Denver and The Muppets. Last year they got Lucas to chime in for certain parts of the "Twelve Days of Christmas." He sang Beaker's "Mimimimimi!" and joined in when they all sang "Badumbumbum!" Bill thought it was a hoot. Jenna loved making him laugh. It always felt just as good as making him proud.

Maybe there's still time. She can play carols while she makes breakfast, and they clean up. Bill Jr. and Lucas are coming over later. Sam won't be over; she'll drop by his mom's house for dessert. Tara's home for winter break.

"It'll be weird to see Bill Jr. now," Julie says. "Now that I know."

Jenna looks up, startled. Julie never initiates this particular conversation. "I don't think he'll say anything," she says quickly, and then she hesitates. "Actually, I have no idea what he'll say."

Julie groans. "I guess it's a good thing Mom's not here."

"I've been thinking about that," Jenna says, gathering the used wrapping paper into a pile. "I think when Mom gets back from her trip, it's time to tell her."

"No."

"No?" Jenna hugs the torn paper in a bundle at her chest and stands up.

Julie shakes her head slowly. Her face struggles for composure.

"This isn't good for us. Any of us. Bill wouldn't have wanted it to be this way."

Julie takes a deep breath and lets it out evenly. "You do whatever you need to do. I don't want to be any part of it."

"Julie—"

"Leave me out of it!" Her face is flushed, and Jenna knows she's right on the edge of tears. Once she starts crying, the entire day will be shot. She'll shut herself in her room and emerge hours later as though nothing had happened. Jenna will be left to clean the house all by herself.

"Okay," Jenna says, literally backing away toward the kitchen. "Eggs?"

***

If Barbara had been home, Bill Jr. never would have suggested it. If Lucas hadn't been asleep upstairs, Jenna never would have agreed. That, and the tension she'd felt all evening, the way Julie had been acting.

Jenna smoked pot a few times in college, nothing ever coming as close to the high she got the first time. Someone made a bong out of a plastic water bottle and a hollowed-out Bic. She spent what felt like half an hour explaining to Liam the Doritos she was eating had never tasted so good. He wasn't ready to give up the bag of potato chips. When they finally traded, they were amazed by the new flavors.

Jenna kept insisting it felt like a movie was being shown inside her mouth. On a projector.

Jenna doesn't know if Julie's ever smoked pot before. They never discuss sex or drugs. Bill Jr. lights the joint and hands it off to Annie, who hands it to Jenna. She can feel Julie's eyes on her, probably wondering the same thing. Jenna takes a small hit and passes it to Julie who inhales deeply and then collapses on the couch in a coughing fit. She skips her next turn.

"I don't get this whole name thing with Lucas. I can't get used to it," Julie sighs, laying her head back.

"Me too," Jenna adds. "I hate change."

Bill Jr. shrugs. "Everything changes." He sucks the end of the joint, holds his breath. "Life is change," he says, nodding slightly to himself.

Jenna rolls her eyes. "That's not true. Some things don't change. Some things are constants." She takes the joint from Annie.

"Like what?" Bill Jr. asks. "What is constant? Give me an example."

Jenna inhales. Her lungs ache. "Bill was a constant."

"Was." Bill Jr. smiles, not unkindly.

"That's different. Bill didn't change; he died." She gives the joint to Julie and tucks her feet underneath her.

"He changed and then he died," Julie says and Jenna glares at her. It's true, of course. He wasn't himself for those last two years. But still, he was the parent Jenna counted on to be there, to answer the phone, to listen. To care. He was dependable, solid, and constant.

"Death is a kind of change." Bill Jr. talks on the inhale. "Don't you think?"

Jenna doesn't answer. She wants to say Bill's love transcends death and isn't changed by it. She passes on the next hit. She wants to be clear headed when she goes to Sam's later.

"You can call him Lucas," Annie says, and Jenna is grateful for the redirection. "'A rose by any other name' and all that."

***

Barbara calls from Cozumel. She asks to speak with Lucas, but when they put him on, he gets quiet. Jenna busies herself with the dishes and ends up being the last to take the phone.

Barbara has a lot to say about the weather and steers clear of stories about Doug, although Jenna imagines him sitting nearby in short shorts and a golf visor, drinking something blue. In all of Barbara's anecdotes, his pretend absence is almost laughable; she's snorkeling and riding a Vespa and tanning by the pool. Jenna knows she would never do any of these things on her own.

"Have you heard from the *biological*?" she asks.

"He didn't even send a card." Jenna shrugs in the empty kitchen, her apathy for no one to see.

Barbara sighs audibly. "The *biological* has been a disappointment on every front. But you had a father. Bill was your father. That's how you should think of it."

"You're right, Mom. That is how I should think of it."

***

They don't take the tree down until after New Year's. Jenna's surprised when Julie offers help. This is the worst of the Christmas jobs, part of the inevitable holiday hangover. Jenna's relieved to have the holidays over with, but survival is a small comfort. The bleak winter looms ahead, the passing of time one more thing that's out of her control.

The handmade school projects are hidden at the back of the tree: The clothespin reindeer and pipe cleaner snowflakes and the felt evergreen with colored popcorn kernels for lights. Their favorite ornaments are featured prominently at eye level, close to a lit bulb. She places them back in the cardboard box, the one with the little dividers, each glass ball nestled in immovable safety. But she sets one ornament aside: A Santa Clause figure with a spring for a neck, a bulbous red clown nose, and wild white hair. No one could ever remember where it came from. Santa on Crack, Jenna had called it once in middle school. She remembers the fluttering in her stomach as she waited to see how the joke would go over if the drug reference would be considered inappropriate. Bill laughed though, and the name stuck.

Jenna tucks the ornament in her winter coat pocket. She'll pack it with her things later.

She and Julie carry the tree out the front door, scattering pine needles all over the kitchen tiles. Jenna goes backward down the front stairs, sweeping her foot behind her with each tentative step. "You're going too fast," she says to Julie.

"It's heavy." "Well, don't drop it." Jenna holds her breath until she feels the solid pavement of the driveway under her feet.

They release their burden at the edge of the road next to the trash cans. The rest of the neighbors have done the same thing. There are browning pines lying like dead bodies up and down the street.

Jenna trudges back up the stairs. When she gets inside, Julie's already tugging the vacuum cleaner down the hall, its electrical cord trailing noisily. Norman scurries up the hall, away. He's always been terrified of the vacuum.

"Mom's coming back Friday," Julie says, fussing with the outlet without looking up.

"Yep."

"When are you moving back to school?"

"This weekend. Liam already moved his stuff in."

Julie looks up from a crouched position. "Do you think I could stay with you for a while?"

Jenna sighs, putting all of Julie's helpfulness into this new context. She wants something. "What's awhile?"

"I don't know. I need to get out of here. Before Friday." She stands and leans against the wall. "I can sleep on the couch."

Jenna pictures this. Julie will be asleep in the living room when she and Liam start their days, demanding quiet. She'll leave glasses and bowls encrusted with dried oatmeal all around the apartment. She'll suggest ordering pizza and have no money to kick in. Her vague *awhile* will turn into weeks. There will be tension with Liam and a confrontation, forcing Julie to leave.

Jenna fingers the ornament in her pocket. "I'm not sure it's a good idea."

Julie crosses her arms, pouting. She's wearing a sweatshirt with the name of their high school disintegrating across the front. The *M* has nearly faded completely, reminding Jenna of a neon sign with a light out.

"If you want to move out, you're going to need to be able to pay rent. You need a plan. Have you thought about what you want to do, you know, with your life?" Jenna steps back and hoists herself up onto the counter.

"My life, Jenna? That's a big question, don't you think?"

"I do."

Julie huffs. "I need to get out of here!" She tosses her head back, hitting the wall. She does this two more times and then looks across the room at Jenna, pointedly. "Can't you help me?"

"I'd like to. I'm not sure how."

"I told you how!" Julie stands up straight, throwing her hands up. "All you have to do is say yes."

Jenna sees the desperation in her sister's face. She understands it. Julie isn't ready to face their mother, to decide what the truth will mean. "I'm sorry," Jenna says. She's looking in her lap, hand in her pocket.

Julie scuffs her foot against the floor, kicking at the pine needles. "Fine." She turns and stomps out of the room, up the stairs, leaving the vacuuming to Jenna.

Chapter Fourteen

Helen Reed lives in a large Victorian house three blocks from campus. The front walk is lined with hedges, the kind with flattop haircuts, and they're covered in a thin blanket of fresh snow. It has been flurrying all morning. There's a brass knocker on the front door, but Jenna uses her knuckles.

The woman who opens the door is not Helen Reed. She has wild, curly red hair and wears a long purple dress with bare feet. "You must be Jenna," she says, smiling warmly and gesturing to come inside. "I'm Toni. Let me take your coat." She hangs it on a coat rack at the bottom of the stairs and puts a hand on the banister. "Helen!"

Toni leads her through the living room. Jenna registers the two matching linen sofas, a glass coffee table and a framed print of calla lilies. She thinks it's Georgia O'Keefe.

Toni holds open a door and Jenna steps inside. "Can I get you a drink?"

"No, thank you," Jenna says, not wanting to be a bother.

"Okay then." Toni smiles again. "She'll be right down."

Alone in the room, Jenna considers sitting down but doesn't. The bookcases are ceiling high and full. Jenna wanders, touching spines and reading the titles. In Professor Reed's office at school, it's all Mill, Kant, Foucault. Here, she has Friedan, Faludi, and Simone de Beauvoir. A whole section of Noam Chomsky. Has Professor Reed read all these books?

Jenna decides someday she'll have a room like this one.

There are more pictures here too. Nearly a dozen framed photographs. One is Helen Reed with Gloria Steinem. Balloon strings are dangling behind them, and Jenna can't tell if it's from a book signing or a birthday party. She can imagine the two of them might be personal friends.

In a beach photograph of Helen and Toni, Helen's wearing a black T-shirt, but the photo cuts off at the waist, and Jenna can't tell if she has shorts on.

She picks up a frame of Helen with her two daughters, one in a cap and gown. She feels a vague jealousy of these women, growing up with such a *force* as a guide in life. What must it be like to have Helen Reed as a mother?

Jenna's startled when the door opens. She places the frame down quickly and stutters a greeting.

She's surprised further when Professor Reed hugs her. "I was sorry to hear about your dad," she says. All Jenna can do in response is nod her head. "You got my letter?"

"I did." Jenna found it days after the funeral, in the stack of envelopes she hadn't wanted to open. The return address was written in loping cursive unlike the notes she wrote on exams: Compact lines slanted to the right.

"My father died when I was a senior in college," Helen says, sitting down behind her desk. "It's a hard time to lose a parent." She shrugs. "There's never a good time."

Jenna sits across from her. "No," she agrees, glumly. She has followed this useless train of thought more than she'd like to admit. Would it have been better to lose him earlier? Certainly not. To never have had him in her life at all, sparing the present pain? Not even for that. Later, though. Later always seems like it might have been better.

Helen smiles sadly. "When my father died, we'd been estranged for over a year. There was much I wished we'd had time to work through together. It took me years to realize none of it mattered. If we'd had more time, we would have worked it out. Not having the time doesn't change that."

Jenna realizes Helen has teared up. She doesn't know what to say.

"What I mean to say," Helen blinks quickly, "is that it does get better."

"Thanks."

"But you'll always miss him." She fingers a leaf of the wilting plant on her desk, frowning.

"I know. I miss him a lot."

Helen sighs. She snaps off the brown leaf and tosses it into a small trash can at the edge of her desk. "You're ready to come back to us next semester?"

"Looks like it."

"Excellent." The paperwork is already on the desk in front of her. She fills it in and signs the bottom. "You're all set." She pushes the paper toward Jenna. "Now, all we need to do is fill out your course selection form." Helen pulls out that semester's catalogue. The stack of yellow paper is about twenty pages thick, stapled in the top left-hand corner; it's a small school.

They plan a credit-heavy semester. This way, Jenna can attend graduation in May and finish her classes during the summer. It's hard to imagine that day, the possibility of her own cap and gown photograph thrown into doubt. Will Julie and Jenna link arms with their mother and smile for the camera? By May? Ever again?

This morning, Julie was up early filling her car with boxes. She's going north to stay with Grammy for *a while*. Clearly, Julie thinks her grandmother will be a refuge, an escape. Jenna suspects Grammy will have stronger notions of how to help her granddaughter with her pre-life crisis. She likes to think of Gram with a project, not so alone. It will be good for them both.

And she can't quite describe the relief of having Julie safely delivered to someone else's care.

"Are you taking my Political Ethics seminar?" Helen asks. "It's filling up fast, but I saved you a spot."

Jenna smiles. "You did?"

"Of course."

Jenna's awestruck with gratitude at simply being thought of. "Thanks so much, Helen. Count me in."

***

When Jenna gets home, she finds her mother sitting at the kitchen table with an open bottle of wine and an empty glass clasped between both hands. Her winter coat has slid off the back of her chair and puddled onto the floor. Her suitcase sits in the doorway as if stalled on its way down the hall.

Barbara's hair is frizzy and puffed out on one side. She looks up when Jenna steps into the room, wide-eyed. Her eye makeup is smudged, and her face is puffy and red from too much sun.

"Mom?"

"Welcome home," Barbara says, wiggling in her seat, pulling her drooping sweater back over her shoulders.

"Yeah. Welcome home." Jenna sits at the table's longer side, her mother at the head. "How was your trip?"

"It was fine," Barbara says, refilling her wine glass.

Jenna looks at her wrist. It's just after three p.m. "Really?"

Barbara shrugs and takes a long sip. "I ended things with Doug. Or he ended things. In the airport, before the flight home."

"Aw, Mom. I'm sorry." And she is, sort of. She's surprised she can still feel sorry for her mother.

"We were on the same flight back. He sat three rows ahead of me. Chatted with the woman next to him the whole way."

"Yuck." And at the same time, the knot forming in Jenna's stomach on the drive home has begun to unravel. She won't have to talk yet about Bill and infidelity and DNA tests. She's letting herself off the hook. Now is not the time.

"I had some cocktails on the flight. Took a cab home."

Jenna nods sympathetically. Definitely not the time.

Barbara holds up her glass. "Alone, again!" She smiles crookedly and finishes the contents in one gulp.

Jenna isn't sure how to respond to this. What she hears is her mother drawing a parallel between losing her husband and losing *Doug*. She sits in her chair. "There are worse things," she tries.

"Worse than being alone?"

Jenna shrugs. "Sometimes being alone can be a good thing. Can be helpful."

Barbara waves her hand in the air, dismissively. She pours another glass.

The gesture only makes Jenna more adamant. "I'm serious," she says. "Maybe you should spend a little more time on your own before you start dating again. Maybe you were rushing it."

Barbara stops pouring, setting the bottle down noisily, her glass only half full. She meets Jenna's gaze. "See, you think Bill died last month. But he didn't."

In the breath Barbara takes before her next sentence, Jenna feels a chill creeping up her back. She closes her eyes, unable to stop her mother from saying the rest.

"The truth is," Barbara continues, "he died two years ago, after the first surgery. We lost him then. The man we brought home was not my husband."

"Don't say that." Jenna's mouth is dry.

"The man we brought home was a doddering idiot."

"Shut up!" Jenna stands, bumping the table and knocking the wineglass over. The bottle rocks in place.

Barbara watches the path of the spilled wine spread across the table and splash onto the kitchen floor. Bill laid the tile all by himself, on his hands and knees.

Jenna sits down. The dripping of the wine is audible.

"I shouldn't have said that," Barbara says. She reaches out an unsteady hand and dips her finger in the dark ribbon of wine on the table. "But you have no right to judge me. You don't know how to put yourself in another person's shoes."

"I don't?"

"It's not the same for you. For you and Julie. It's not the same quality of grief." She licks her finger absently.

Jenna's shaking. Quality of grief? She wants to pour the rest of the wine in her mother's lap, bash her over the head with the empty bottle. She wants to remind her mother that when Bill got sick, no one took over for him. She and Julie had been orphans for the last two years. She wants to say she came home to take care of him because no one else was doing it. She wants to scream at her mother for abandoning him. Abandoning all of them. But she doesn't trust her voice.

Jenna slides her chair back and stands up slowly. She walks to the kitchen counter, disconnects the roll of paper towels from the rod and tosses it at her mother. The roll bounces across the table and lands on the floor. "He was my father!"

Unfazed, Barbara bends to pick it up. "I know."

"No." Jenna slaps the table and leans in, looking into her mother's startled face. "He was my *father*."

Silence. Barbara examines Jenna's face carefully. She swallows and looks away, ripping off a long stream of paper towels. "I don't know what you mean," she says, but her voice is small, and her hands are trembling.

Jenna watches as the wine spreads slowly into the paper cloth in ever widening red circles. "Bill told me before he died."

Barbara focuses on the spill. "Bill told you what?" she says, without looking up.

Jenna sits down at the table again. She remembers Bill's face when he said it, the way he held his hands open to show how he had held them as babies, how his voice buckled with regret for leaving them. For doing as he was told.

"Bill was our father. Our biological father."

Barbara's eyes flit around the room. Jenna can see her weighing her options, deciding whether she can talk her way out of it. She chews her bottom lip. "I shouldn't have had so much to drink," she says in a whisper, as if to herself, rubbing her forehead. "I can't think straight."

Jenna crosses her arms and doesn't speak.

Barbara's head jerks to attention. "Did you tell Julie?"

"Of course."

"Jenna!" she says, scolding, as if she has the right. "Where is she?"

"Gone. She'll tell you where she is if she wants you to know. I won't speak for her." This part is rehearsed. It's what Jenna has decided is fair.

Barbara's jaw goes slack, turning her mouth into a little circle. "You've known all these months?"

Jenna nods.

"Why didn't you say anything?"

This makes Jenna angry, as if the issue at hand is how Barbara has been left out of the loop. She remembers Sam asking if part of her enjoyed having a secret from her mother. At the time, she'd said no. But right now, she feels the power of it in her mother's crumpled face, her irrelevant hurt feelings.

Barbara seems to be waiting for an answer as she sifts through her memories and they take on new shape, colored by this knowledge.

"I've been busy," Jenna says, sneering.

Barbara brings her hands up, pressing her fingers to her temples. "You can go ahead and judge me if you want to. I met my soulmate while I was married to someone else. You don't know the kind of anguish I went through."

"It's not about judging you," Jenna snaps. "God. It's not about you! Didn't you think we had a right to know? Julie and me? He was our father!"

"He was always your father in every way that counted. What would have changed?"

"What would have changed? Are you serious?" Jenna yells. "Our medical histories, for one. All those summer bus trips to Ohio to visit a man we thought was our father. We grew up feeling like we didn't matter to him, desperate to make some kind of connection. But he wasn't our father." She pauses. "Did he know?"

Barbara shakes her head. "I never told anyone."

"Except Bill."

"Bill just knew. The timing."

"And the *biological*?" Jenna makes finger quotes in the air. "He never suspected?"

"You were tiny. He assumed you were early."

"We weren't?

"Not as early as he thought."

"Then why were we so small?"

Barbara rakes her fingers through her hair in an apparent attempt to tame it. "It was a tough time for me. I wasn't taking the best care of myself." Her hair becomes wild with static electricity and gets worse the more she touches it.

Jenna feels queasy. "Of yourself? You mean you weren't taking care of us." Jenna pushes her chair away from the table. "At least you're consistent."

"I need to lie down."

Jenna realizes she isn't going to get an apology. "Do Julie and I have the same father?"

Barbara scowls, seeming not to understand.

"It can happen," Jenna explains, and she takes a certain pleasure in saying the rest. "If a woman has sex with two men within a few days of each other, twins can have different fathers."

Barbara stares at her. She does look tired. Her face sags, giving away her age as her jaw dissolves into her neck.

"It's like what happens with *dogs*."

Her mother flinches. It's the first time Jenna has gotten the response she's after. "It's not possible."

"How did you pass us off as another man's kids if that's not possible?"

"I told you."

The problem is her mother can't be trusted.

Jenna grips the edge of the table, turning her knuckles white. "You need to know," she says, struggling to keep her voice even, "you didn't only hurt us. Julie and me. You hurt Bill. Making him keep this secret."

"We decided together." Barbara gathers the crumpled wet towels into a pile in front of her. "You don't understand. Things were different back then. I was married to a deeply religious man."

"But that was years ago. Why keep up the lie?"

"It was easier."

"Easier for who?" *For whom*, Bill would correct.

Barbara doesn't answer. It wasn't easier for Julie or Jenna, who had never questioned Bill's love for them, but imagined he'd had to cultivate it and accept them as part of a package deal. Knowing his love for them was as much a part of him as they were changed things.

And it certainly wasn't easier for Bill. He'd been tortured by it. Even in his last days, when everything had been muddled, he longed to claim them.

Jenna gets to her feet. "Don't forget to clean up the rest of your mess," she says, gesturing to the wine on the floor. She gets Norman's leash, and he comes trotting down the hall at the sound of metal against metal, the precise intonation.

"Where are you going?" Barbara asks, sounding suddenly frantic.

"None of your business," Jenna answers and she takes the front steps two at a time, pulling Norman behind her.

***

Jenna gets out of the car because Norman starts whining as soon as the engine stops. She sits on Sam's front steps, unsure if Norman's allowed in the house. Her fingers are numb inside her gloves. Norman strains at the end of the leash, lifts his leg and turns the slush yellow. He trots back, settling at her feet. By the time Sam's car pulls into the driveway, the snow falls in earnest.

"Forget your keys?" he asks, walking toward her.

"I brought a friend."

"Well, any friend of yours," he begins, winking. "You okay?"

Jenna stands to let him by. He slides his key into the lock. "My mom's home," she says. Sam looks at her over his shoulder. "Oh." Norman's pressing his nose against the door and when Sam pushes it open, he charges inside. Jenna lets go of the leash.

Inside, Sam takes her coat and brushes the light dusting of snow from her hair. "What did she have to say for herself?"

"Oh, you know," Jenna throws her hands up. "It's not her fault. Everything was hard for her, and knowing the truth wouldn't have changed anything anyway."

"Right." Sam shakes his head back and forth several times, his sandy hair sliding across his forehead. "Wow. I'm sorry."

Jenna groans. "Not your fault."

"Still."

They'd said these words when they were beginning to know each other.

Norman comes back into the kitchen, having completed his inspection of the apartment. He's dragging the leash behind him and Sam bends to unhook it. He scratches the top of Norman's head and Norman allows it, leaning into it, unable to conceal his enjoyment.

"Want a dog?" Jenna asks, mostly joking.

Still crouched on the floor, Sam looks up. His eyebrows lift.

"I haven't figured out what to do with him. My mom's never home. They don't allow dogs at the apartment."

Sam takes fistfuls of Norman's neck fur and looks into his eyes. "What would you think about that, buddy?"

"I wasn't serious," Jenna says quickly. She pushes her hair out of her eyes.

"Why not?" Sam stands.

"You don't want a dog," Jenna tells him.

"Do you have another plan?

"No."

"I could do this," he says, but there's a question in his tone. "Let me do this," he says, sounding more certain this time. He touches Jenna's wrist.

She tilts her head, looking at him through lowered lids. He's so beautiful and generous. She reaches toward him and touches his chest with her fingertips. He pulls her in and holds her close. "Are you sure?" she whispers, her lips grazing the rough stubble of his neck.

"Mmhmm," he murmurs into her hair. "So, do you feel better? Getting it off your chest?"

She perches her chin on his shoulder and exhales as he moves his hands slowly up and down her back. "Better? I don't know yet. Maybe relieved."

"Yeah." Sam clasps his hands over her rump. "Better might take some time."

They stand in the kitchen, embracing. Jenna wilts against his chest, exhaustion draining from her limbs. She does feel changed somehow, though it's hard to articulate. The confrontation with her mother has been weighing heavily on her for weeks, maybe months. It was like worrying she'd left the oven on or had forgotten to do her homework. Looming on the horizon constantly, like a dreaded to-do list that never got done.

But now it's done. She's free to focus on other things.

"You know what I'd like?" she asks him.

"What's that?" He's still holding her, Norman panting expectantly at their feet.

"I'd like to go lie down and give you my full attention."

Sam pulls away so he can look in her eyes. He cocks an eyebrow at her. They smile at each other, and she traces those starburst lines along the sides of his face.

Jenna and Norman will sleep over that night, to ease him into his new home. It won't occur to her to run it by her mother. In the morning, when Jenna picks up her things at the house, she'll get Norman's bowls, his big bag of dry food, the three toys he hardly cares about. She hopes she won't run into her mother.

She likes to imagine throwing herself into the next few months of school, finding no reason to talk to her mother at all.

Tomorrow, Jenna and Sam will drive to the apartment. He'll help carry her things up those three flights of stairs and they'll get Chinese takeout with Liam.

But tonight is theirs.

Chapter Fifteen

As it turns out, there is a photo of Jenna in her cap and gown, her mother and sister standing on either side, beaming for the camera.

After the flash went off, the two of them walked away in different directions, making room for other photo groupings: Bill Jr. and Annie and Lucas, Gram and Julie, Liam, Sam.

As far as Jenna knows, Julie hasn't spoken to their mother since the Christmas phone call. When Jenna visited her at Grammy's over February break, she tried to advocate further DNA testing, but Julie rolled her eyes.

Jenna searched her face for traces of the biological, for his mother. All she could call to mind was the woman's sunken, dying eyes. If they had different fathers, Julie was still at risk. She'd need to keep writing those words on the medical forms for the rest of her life: Cervical cancer.

"I don't care," Julie said, and Jenna let it drop.

After all the pictures were taken, everyone gathered for a celebratory meal at a Mexican restaurant with a long table. Barbara took a seat between Annie and Liam, the safest choice. Unfortunately, this put her across the table from Grammy. Jenna marveled at the way the two women treated the bowl of chips between them as a sort of Berlin Wall.

Jenna was surprised to see her mother at all, sitting alone during the ceremony, wearing a blue dress and sporting a new haircut. After the graduates tossed their caps in the air, Barbara made her way over, slowly, waiting her turn. Jenna took vague pleasure in this, speaking a bit longer with Helen Reed than she might have otherwise. She held her mother in her peripheral vision, a woman standing quite straight and calling to mind

Hester Prynne. The last time they spoke, awkwardly over the phone, Jenna had downplayed the day's importance. It wasn't real. The rolled-up paper the dean handed her was blank.

She has the real one now, though; the dark leather folder containing her diploma rests on a shelf of the bookcase in Sam's little yellow house. Their place.

She'd moved in officially in September, though she spent most of the summer there, studying for her classes in the tiny backyard, drinking iced tea, and getting brown. The house had no AC, and on extra humid days, Jenna took cold showers. The water would be cool when it hit her head and warm by the time it got to her feet. When Sam got home from work, she'd meet him on the porch and make him take her someplace air conditioned for dinner.

When Jenna told Liam she was hoping to move out before their lease was up, he'd laughed. "Turnabout is fair play," he said.

He was sleeping fine these days, in his own bed, alone. He was making enough money to cover the rent by himself. He wished her well: "That one's a keeper."

And he was. Sam. She knew.

Jenna hears him in the bathroom now, the whir of the electric toothbrush on the other side of the door. When it stops, Jenna calls out, "Julie's coming up on Friday," she reminds him.

The door opens. "Down." "Oh." She gets into bed. "Right."

Sam slides in next to her. In the corner, Norman picks up his head and yawns, then settles his snout back onto his paws. "When's her flight?"

"Saturday evening." Julie was flying to New Orleans to volunteer for Habitat for Humanity. She'd spent the summer with a chapter in Maine. Jenna still has trouble picturing her swinging a hammer on a roof top, sawdust in her hair. At first, she'd suspected there was a guy involved, but Grammy said no.

"Will she see your mother before she goes?"

"Nope." Jenna sits up. She reaches for her book on the nightstand and places it in her lap. "I'm scared for them, but I can't convince her when I'm not doing great myself."

"I think you're doing great." Sam squeezes the back of her neck. His fingers are strong and warm.

In the four months since moving back to the town where her mother lives, Jenna has met her for dinner twice. The Ruby Tuesdays at the mall, a neutral location where neither would be prone to raised voices or displays of emotion. Between the excruciating stretches of silence, they'd talked about Jenna's new job at a community outreach center, how Norman liked his new digs, the weather—topics that didn't lead to dangerous territories. They haven't talked about Julie's whereabouts or Barbara's current dating life. Bill's birthday passed without comment. Jenna wavered from feeling like she was having an overly polite conversation with a stranger to being a sullen adolescent in a standoff. There was no laughter at these dinners, no familiar ease to the exchange.

"How do I forgive her when she isn't sorry?" Jenna asks.

"Just because she can't apologize doesn't mean she isn't sorry."

They've had this conversation before and they'll have it again, many times, perhaps forever. Jenna can't understand why her mother doesn't claim responsibility for what she's done, why she hasn't said the words. It would be simple and cost her nothing.

And why, when Jenna recognizes how small the gesture is—meaningless, really—why does this matter so much?

"Why do I care?"

"She's your mother."

That's what it always comes down to.

In the parking lot after the graduation dinner, Barbara had given Jenna an envelope. She pulled her cardigan closed, protecting against a breeze as the May evening dimmed.

"You've worked very hard," she told Jenna stiffly. "You should be proud."

"Thank you," Jenna said, scuffing a foot against the pavement. "I'm glad you came." And this was true.

Her mother's eyes glistened as she reached out a tentative hand. She tucked the loose strand of hair behind Jenna's ear. "Always will," she said, and she turned, ducking into her car.

She drove away then and Jenna swallowed hard over the lump in her throat. It wouldn't always be this way, she told herself. They had time to work it out.

Sometimes it helped to think of life as short, making the resolution of differences an urgent matter. But in this case, Jenna prefers to consider life is long. Someday, she will look back on this as the year she and her mother were lost to each other, the year they struggled toward forgiveness.

Jenna opens the book in her lap. Unable to cash the check her mother gave her, she uses it as a bookmark.

There would be time.

Acknowledgements

I have been working on this book for a really, really long time. Years ago, when I sent it out to literary agents, one of them told me that she would be interested in reading Barbara's story. At the time, I was in my twenties, and the idea of writing from her perspective seemed extremely foreign. When I wrote *Unclaimed Baggage* I thought Barbara was the villain, but one of the things that happens as we age is that we are able to see the complexities in people. *Reclaimed Baggage* is about those complexities.

I am overwhelmed by the amount of people I need to thank for helping me to write this book over the years: writing classes and writers groups and beta readers and my mom and my editors, especially Mary.

About The Author

Katie grew up in New Hampshire, went to college in Massachusetts, and settled down in Arizona. These are the environments you'll find in her stories because she thinks having an authentic sense of place is so important when you're reading.

She's been calling herself a writer since the second grade when her teacher had the class bind their stories with patterned paper and put them on display in the library. She writes the kind of fiction she likes to read: character-driven, relationship-focused, and emotionally complex. She has published several novels and a collection of short stories.

She's spent the last twenty years in Tucson where she lives with her sweet yellow lab and even sweeter boyfriend.

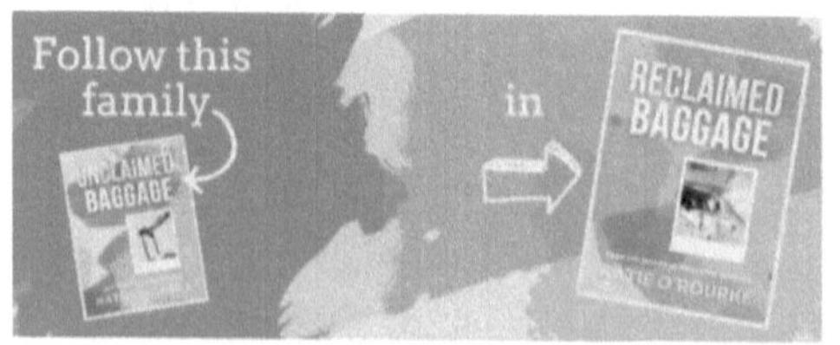

www.ingramcontent.com/pod-product-compliance
Lightning Source LLC
Chambersburg PA
CBHW020145120726
47903CB00007B/2427